The LANDSEEKERS

Center Point
Large Print

Also by Allan Vaughan Elston and available from Center Point Large Print:

Saddle Up for Steamboat
Timberline Bonanza
Treasure Coach from Deadwood

This Large Print Book carries the Seal of Approval of N.A.V.H.

The LANDSEEKERS

Allan Vaughan ELSTON

CENTER POINT LARGE PRINT
THORNDIKE, MAINE

This Center Point Large Print edition
is published in the year 2018 by arrangement with
Golden West Literary Agency.

First US edition: Lippincott.
First UK edition: Ward Lock.

The text of this Large Print edition is unabridged.
In other aspects, this book may vary
from the original edition.
Printed in the United States of America
on permanent paper.
Set in 16-point Times New Roman type.

ISBN: 978-1-68324-760-9 (hardcover)
ISBN: 978-1-68324-764-7 (paperback)

Library of Congress Cataloging-in-Publication Data

Names: Elston, Allan Vaughan, 1887-1976 author.
Title: The landseekers / Allan Vaughan Elston.
Description: Center Point Large Print edition. | Thorndike, Maine :
    Center Point Large Print, 2018.
Identifiers: LCCN 2017061797| ISBN 9781683247609
    (hardcover : alk. paper) | ISBN 9781683247647 (pbk. : alk. paper)
Subjects: LCSH: Large type books. | GSAFD: Western stories.
Classification: LCC PS3509.L77 L36 2018 | DDC 813/.6—dc23
LC record available at https://lccn.loc.gov/2017061797

To the old *Tri-Weekly Statesman* of Boise City—
a sleeping history in the archives of Idaho, from
whose early files come a little of the fact and
much of the background for this book.

The
LANDSEEKERS

A story of Idaho in the year 1879—when goldseekers were thinning out and landseekers came to replace them, wheeling westward singly and in caravans along the Overland Trail.

CHAPTER I

Salisbury, Hailey and Company's Overland stage, rolling northwesterly toward Oregon, was on time to the minute and due in Boise City by midafternoon. Of its five passengers, only two had ridden all the way from the railhead at Kelton, Utah. One of these was a brown-eyed girl of nineteen, delicately pretty in spite of her travel weariness. She tried to speak cheerfully to a lady who shared the seat with her. "It will be wonderful to sleep in a bed again, Mrs. Lindsay."

Nan Stanley had left Kelton at noon Monday. It was now eleven o'clock Wednesday morning. Since she'd boarded it the coach had changed horses seventeen times and had used five drivers. The present driver, Dan Harbison, had come on at the breakfast stop, a swing station called Rattlesnake.

Lois Lindsay, who'd boarded the stage at Rattlesnake, showed no weariness at all. She looked at Nan with a gentle sympathy. "You poor child! Sitting up two nights like that! How long will you be in Boise City?"

"Until my two brothers get there," Nan said. "They've got three hundred cows and a wagon-load of household goods. They plan to start the drive from Kelton tomorrow. How long will it take them, do you suppose?"

Mrs. Lindsay didn't know. But Jim Agnew, one of the two male passengers sitting opposite them, had an answer. "It's two hundred and sixty miles, Miss. If your brothers are smart they won't try to make more'n twelve mile a day. Grazin' 'em along easy like that they can keep their stuff fat. At that rate it'd take 'em about three weeks to make Boise City."

"You won't mind waiting three weeks at the Overland," Mrs. Lindsay said. "It's the most comfortable hotel in Idaho. I'll see that you meet some nice people."

"You live at the Overland yourself?" Nan asked.

"Not now. But once I worked as ticket clerk for Wells Fargo. The Boise City office of Wells Fargo is in the Overland lobby. That was a long, long time ago . . ." A look of sad reminiscence came to Lois Lindsay's face and she withdrew into a shell of silence.

It couldn't have been so very long ago, Nan thought. Mrs. Lindsay didn't look a day over thirty-three. During the four-hour ride since leaving Rattlesnake Nan had already learned from the general talk that Lois Lindsay had been a widow for ten years and was a woman of considerable property, some of it invested in Boise City bank stock and some of it in a mine at

Rocky Bar. A branch stage line from Rocky Bar joined the Overland road at Rattlesnake and Mrs. Lindsay was returning from an inspection of that mine.

From the same general talk Nan knew that Jim Agnew, a genial Boise City liveryman and horse trader, had just sold forty horses at Rocky Bar and was returning home by stage. Of the other male passenger inside the stage Nan knew nothing except that his name was Rogan and that he'd ridden the coach all the way from Kelton. The man had a fleshy, unshaven face and whisky breath. Right now he was soddenly asleep.

The fifth passenger was a drygoods drummer named Abbott who'd boarded at Glenn's Ferry, where the road crossed the Snake River. He was riding up front with the driver.

"How many more times," Nan asked, "do we change horses?"

"Only once, at Dunn's station," Agnew told her. "Oughta be there in an hour. Mind if I smoke, ladies?"

The cigar was in his mouth, but before he could light it the coach stopped with a jolt so abrupt that Nan Stanley was thrown forward against the liveryman's knees. Rogan came awake, blinking stupidly, and they all heard rough voices.

"Sounds like a hold-up," Agnew whispered.

Nan looked out and saw three mounted men.

They were masked and aiming rifles at the coach. A shotgun clattered on the ground as the driver threw it down. Two of the masked men had tall, thin builds. The other was heavyset. "Just don't get funny," the stocky man said, "and nobody'll get hurt."

Nan saw Agnew hide a fat wallet under the cushion of his seat. It would be the money paid him at Rocky Bar for the forty horses. "Everybody out," the stocky robber shouted, "and line up."

Taking a cue from the liveryman, Nan Stanley slipped her purse under a seat cushion. "It won't do any good," Lois Lindsay said. The older woman kept her purse in hand as she got out of the coach, followed by Nan, Agnew and Rogan.

By then Harbison and Abbott were standing at a forewheel, hands raised. The thickset robber dismounted and slapped the pockets of Agnew and Rogan to make sure they weren't armed. Nan, dismayed rather than frightened, took a stand at the driver's elbow with Mrs. Lindsay on the other side of her. Agnew, Rogan and Abbott lined up at Harbison's left.

One of the lean robbers climbed to the front boot. He came down with two padlocked leather bags, one containing registered mail and the other Wells Fargo express. "Dump everything in the sack," the head robber ordered.

The taller of the thin robbers held a grain sack

open, and into it were dropped the two leather bags. The other thin man took wallets from Rogan, Abbott and Harbison, and a purse from Mrs. Lindsay. He tossed them into the grain sack, then stepped into the coach. When he came out he had a grin on the part of his face which showed below the mask. In his hands were Agnew's wallet and Nan's purse.

"It's all I've got!" Nan murmured to Mrs. Lindsay. Her brothers had given her a hundred dollars to pay hotel expenses while she waited for them at Boise City.

Lois Lindsay squeezed her hand. "Don't worry, my dear. You can stay at my house if you like."

The tallest highwayman lugged the bulging grain sack to his horse. He was hoisting it to his saddle when a rifle shot stopped him. It cracked from the brushy brow of a hillock about two hundred yards north of the road.

The man with the loot sack gave a yell and dropped it. He stood nursing a bloody arm while the other two robbers whipped up rifles and fired toward the hillock. The only thing they could see to shoot at was a puff of smoke. Then a second shot left a smoke puff a few steps to the right of the first. Either two riflemen were firing from the brush or one rifleman was nimbly shifting his position. The second shot tipped the stocky bandit's hat back on his head and Nan saw a hole through it.

"Grab that sack, Slim, and let's ride!"

The head robber fired twice again but with no target except smoke puffs. The man with the bleeding arm scrambled into his saddle while the third robber picked up the sack. It was bulky and awkward to handle. He got a boot in his stirrup when another shot from the hillock brought a squeal from his horse. The bullet had nicked the animal's ear and made it shy with a suddenness that dumped both sack and rider to the ground.

By then both the other robbers were asaddle and making off.

The third man was left alone with a hard choice. He could abandon the loot sack, mount unencumbered and ride off, or he could pick up the sack and try to mount with it, all the while needing at least one hand to shoot with in case the four male passengers made a dive for him. Two of them, the driver and the liveryman, looked ready to try it bare-handed.

Another shot from the hillock decided it. The bullet kicked dust under the already frightened horse and made it shy again. Lest it get too far out of his reach and leave him stranded, the third robber made a run for it. He jumped into his saddle and raced off after his companions.

Jim Agnew turned with a wry grin to Mrs. Lindsay. "I had two thousand bucks on me, Lois, and I was about to kiss it goodbye."

Dan Harbison picked up his shotgun and spoke

sheepishly to Nan. "Sorry, Miss. They had me covered before I even saw 'em."

"Look!" Nan exclaimed, pointing. "Our rescuer!"

The mounted cowboy who came riding toward them wore a high-crowned, cream-colored hat and a doeskin jacket. Between the jacket and the hat brim were three shades of red—the russet red of his hair, the sunburned red of his face and the crimson red of the bandana knotted at his throat. The butt plate of a rifle showed at his saddle scabbard and a gun-weighted holster rode on his thigh. His mount, big and roan and high-headed, came clicking up with a nice, singlefoot gait.

"Hope those fellas didn't make off with anything," the rider said as he drew up. He had blue eyes and they fixed brightly on Nan Stanley. "You ain't hurt any, are you?"

"Not at all," Nan assured him. "Thank you very much."

"And not a nickel lost," Agnew added jubilantly. He went to the grain sack and shook everything out of it. After reclaiming his own wallet he handed the other items back to their owners.

The outlaws, who'd headed obliquely into a belt of cottonwoods along Indian Creek, were far gone now. They'd quickly lose their tracks in the creek riffles. "Reckon there's no use chasin' 'em," the cowboy said. At close range he seemed barely more than twenty-one years old.

"Of course not," Mrs. Lindsay agreed. "We can report them to the sheriff at Boise City. Were you going that way, Mister . . . ?"

"Hallam," the cowboy said. "I'm Verne Hallam of Kansas, ma'am, on my way to Oregon." His wide, good-natured face had a grin on it. "It's likely your sheriff'll want to ask me a few questions, seein' as I did some of the powder burning."

"Lucky for us you did," Nan said gratefully.

"We've got a meal stop at Dunn's," Harbison told him, "about five miles up the road."

"I'll get my pack," Verne Hallam said, "and join you there." Abruptly he wheeled his horse and rode north, disappearing over the low, brushy ridge. Presumably he had a camp and a pack kit beyond it.

In a few minutes the four-horse coach was rattling on toward its next relay stop. They crossed Indian Creek and in an hour came to the old Charlie Black farmstead recently taken over by Jimmie Dunn. Dunn himself stood on the porch pounding a dinner gong. "Come and get it," he invited as they got out of the stage.

"Set another plate, Jimmie," Agnew said. "We've got a friend on horseback right behind us."

Hostlers appeared to change the stage horses

and the passengers went inside. They were still eating when the cowboy from Kansas rode up, leading a pack mare. The seat saved for him was beside Nan Stanley.

Before taking it the cowboy spoke to Dunn. "Got a forge here? My horse just threw a shoe."

"Sure," Dunn said, "and one of my hostlers used to be a blacksmith. He'll be busy, though, for the next few hours. If you want to stay all night I've got a bunk for you. You could ride on to Boise City in the morning."

"I'll do that," Verne Hallam decided. "That pack mare of mine's pretty well played out and she can use a day's rest. Thanks."

He hung his hat and gunbelt on a rack and sat down by Nan. Mrs. Lindsay made the introductions. "This is Nan Stanley, Mr. Hallam. She's on her way to Boise City to wait for a cattle drive due there. I'm Lois Lindsay. Left to right, these gentlemen are Mr. Jim Agnew, Boise City liveryman, Dan Harbison, stage driver, Mr. Abbott of Denver, and Mr. Lew Rogan, who when I first knew him twelve years ago was a constable at Idaho City."

"Pleased to meet you, folks. Me, I'm thirty days out of Kansas and they tell me it's still a long piece to Oregon. I'm looking for a good cow country and they say I won't find one this side of Umatilla. Stopped last night at Soul's Rest."

The stage had changed horses at a relay station

called Soul's Rest about three hours after leaving Rattlesnake, Nan remembered. "We were just checking our memories, Mr. Hallam," she said, "about those three robbers. One was short and stocky; two were tall and lean; two rode bay horses and one had a white-stockinged black. Did you notice anything else?"

"I sure did," Hallam said, helping himself to a hot biscuit. "The stocky man had black eyes and a flat nose and his forehead had a slash scar slanting down to the left."

The others stared at him. "But how could you tell?" Agnew wondered. "He was masked and you were two hundred yards away."

"Not when I first saw 'em," the Kansan corrected. "I left Soul's Rest about eight o'clock and was getting close to a cottonwood creek about ten-thirty."

"That would be Indian Creek," Mrs. Lindsay interposed, "where we were held up. You mean you saw the men waiting there?"

"I saw three faces peerin' out of a gully near the trail. They didn't know I saw 'em and I didn't stop. They could have been campers or tramps. So I rode on and crossed the creek. Then I got to thinkin'. I knew this was a stage road. When I left Soul's Rest the hostlers were getting fresh horses ready for a stage due pretty soon. That stage would be about half an hour behind me. Maybe those three jiggers aimed to hold it up."

"So you doubled back?" Agnew prompted.

"I circled back, keeping out of sight. Left my horse and mare in some junipers, took my rifle and slipped up on 'em from behind. Time I got into position the show had already started. May I thank you for that honey, Miss Stanley?"

Nan passed him the bowl of honey. "So you're the only one of us," she said, "who saw them unmasked."

"The only one of us," Lois Lindsay agreed, "who can give the sheriff first-hand descriptions."

"Reckon I am, ma'am."

"In that case," Jim Agnew suggested, "you'd better ride the stage with us to Boise City. The sheriff oughta hear what you've got to say, firsthand and fast."

Prompt agreement came from Stationmaster Dunn. "Agnew's right, young man. I can send your horse and pack into town tomorrow. One of my men's going in anyway."

Hallam hesitated. He wasn't in the habit of being separated from his horse, even for a day.

A smile from Nan decided him. "Please, Mr. Hallam. After you've saved our lives and fortunes we don't want to go off and leave you here."

"If you'll quit callin' me Mister I'll go along. Verne's the name. But I'm not through eating yet." He spread honey on another biscuit.

"No hurry," Dan Harbison said. "Won't hurt

us to be a bit late. Fact is we're lucky the Plover gang didn't shoot us up."

Lois Lindsay asked curiously, "What makes you think it was the Plover gang?"

"I didn't," the driver said, "until Verne mentioned a forehead scar. Accordin' to posters I've seen, Floyd Plover tallies out like that. And he's a mean one."

Rogan fixed a squinty gaze on Verne Hallam and spoke for the first time. "Mean enough to get even with you, cowboy. That guy won't sleep good until he's paid you off. It'll burn him up, you chasin' him off a road job after he had the dough all sacked. He's got heelers in Boise City and any one of 'em could slip you a slug first dark night you walk down a street by yourself. If you're smart you'll make a quick report, then keep on goin' and not stop again this side of Umatilla."

A look of concern came to Mrs. Lindsay's face. "He'll read about it in the papers," she said, "and learn that you're the only real witness against him. It's not fair for you to take risks like that, Verne Hallam, when you're just a stranger riding through on your way to Oregon."

Jim Agnew saw the same concern on Nan's face and he broke in with a bluff reassurance. "Verne's pretty good at taking care of himself from what I've seen. And if he needs any help we've got two darned good lawmen to side him. Sheriff Oldham and Deputy U. S. Marshal Orlando Robbins. Nothing they'd like better'n a showdown with the Plover gang." He looked out a window and saw four fresh strong horses hitched to the stage. "Soon as you get enough nourishment, boy, let's all load up and hit for town."

CHAPTER II

Verne went first to the stable to make sure his horse and pack mare were properly curried and grained. He gave instructions about shoeing the roan. Then he took his rifle and slicker roll and hurried up front to board the stage.

To his chagrin he found that the only convenient seat for him was on the box beside the driver. The salesman Abbott, a man of slight build, was seated inside between Rogan and Agnew. Verne Hallam, a big man with a forty-five gun on his thigh, would feel awkwardly intrusive if he squeezed himself in between two ladies.

His disappointment was so transparent that Lois Lindsay, wise to the moods of young men, could hardly miss it. At the table she'd guessed that this young man's consent to go along on the stage had been largely influenced by a desire to get better acquainted with Nan Stanley. She smiled and said gayly: "We'll feel much safer the rest of the way in with you riding on the guard seat, Verne Hallam. Won't we, Nan?"

"Indeed," Nan murmured.

The girl's disappointment was hardly less obvious than Hallam's and Lois Lindsay said brightly: "To celebrate our deliverance I want you and Nan to be my guests for supper at the

Overland. Wade Canby's meeting the stage and we can make a party of it."

"How nice of you!" Nan said.

"It sure is, Mrs. Lindsay." Verne climbed to the seat beside Harbison. A whip cracked and they were off at a gallop toward Boise City.

"It's sixteen miles," the driver said. "We oughta be there by half past four."

"Who's Wade Canby?" Verne asked curiously.

"He's a mining engineer who's slated to marry Mrs. Lindsay about a month from now. Been sparkin' her for years and finally he talked her into it."

"Canby's a Boise City man?"

"He is now. But when he first came to this country, back in the Sixties, he hung out his shingle at Idaho City. Idaho City was boom gold diggings in those days. Long about 1870 the pay gravel up there began thinning out and Canby moved his office thirty-five miles south to Boise."

"Boise City never was a gold town?"

"Not to speak of. Mainly it's a stage and freighting center on the Overland Trail, with branch lines north and south. It's county seat of Ada County and capital of Idaho, so a lot of politickin' goes on there. But if you want a real open-range cow country with big outfits and mixed roundups, you'd better go back to Wyoming or on west to Oregon."

Harbison let his team slow down while a freight wagon passed them, heading for the railroad at Kelton. "The Boise River valley," the driver remarked presently, "has a few good farms and small ranches. The Stanley girl's brothers figure to buy or lease one of 'em and settle there."

"What line was Mrs. Lindsay's husband in?" Verne asked. "Livestock or mining?"

"Marcus Lindsay was a hardrock man. Got himself blasted to smithereens in a mine explosion. That was ten years ago in the summer of '69. They had to dig him out from under about twenty ton of rock and pick him up in pieces. His wife like to never got over it. They say it was more'n five years before she even looked at another man."

"She was living at the mine when it happened?"

"Nope. Wasn't any fit place for a woman to live up there in Squaw Creek Canyon. Just a sod shack Marcus bached in while he drove a test tunnel. To help out Lois got herself a job clerkin' in the Wells Fargo office at Boise City. She was at work in the Overland Hotel lobby when the bad news came. 'Bout seven months after that her son was born and she named him Marcus Junior."

Verne was ready to let the subject drop. But the talkative driver added another detail or two. "Lois tried to sell that Squaw Creek claim but no-one would give her any cash for it. Finally she swapped it for a half interest in a played-out gold mine at Rocky Bar, about a hundred miles east of here. Later the Rocky Bar property hit rich payrock and Lois has been collecting dividends ever since."

"What about this fella Rogan?" Verne asked. "She said he used to be a constable."

"He was a constable at Idaho City back in '67," Harbison remembered, "in the lush days there. The town fired him on suspicion that he took bribes to turn prisoners loose. Then he came to Boise City and has been living by his wits ever since. Two weeks ago he rode my stage on his way to Salt Lake City via Kelton. Told me it was a business trip. A shady business, likely. I doubt if Lew Rogan's turned an honest dollar in ten years."

Another freight outfit met and passed them. The coach rattled along over bare, rolling terrain until off to the north Verne sighted a belt of cottonwoods marking the course of a river. "It's the Boise River," Harbison said. "Flows into the Snake about where the two rivers hit the Oregon line."

The stage road angled obliquely toward the river and soon Verne could see a sizable town on the far side of it. "We cross on a ferry," Dan said.

At the foot of a grade they found the ferry waiting. "Have a good trip, Dan?" the ferryman asked as they drove onto it.

"Fine, Bert, except for a hold-up at Indian Creek."

The river was eighty yards wide and during the slow, cable-guided crossing Harbison gave the ferryman a few details. An emigrant wagon and half a dozen horsemen were also crossing on the ferry and they heard the report. "Want me to tip off the sheriff, Dan?" a rider offered. "I'm going right by the jail."

"Do that, Rufe. Tell him to meet me at the Overland."

The ferry bumped the north bank and landing planks were pushed out. Dan drove his coach off and sent it bumping up the cloddy ruts of Seventh Street. Rufe loped ahead to carry the news of the hold-up to Sheriff Oldham.

At Main Street the stage turned a block west and drew up at the Overland Hotel. It was a long, two-story frame building with a balcony on the Eighth Street side. Always a crowd waited there for the Kelton and Umatilla stages. Today's included a reporter for the *Triweekly Statesman* who stood pad in hand ready to take down names of incoming passengers. Another who waited there was a tall, well-dressed man with bronzed good looks who pushed forward to help Lois Lindsay from the coach. His trimmed mustache and polished puttees gave him a professional appearance and Verne tabbed him for the mining engineer, Wade Canby.

28

By the time all passengers were off the stage Verne saw two men with law badges hurrying down Eighth toward them. Lois Lindsay, after accepting a kiss of greeting from her fiancé, said brightly: "Wade, I want you to meet Nan Stanley. I've invited her to take supper with us along with this nice young man who saved our pocketbooks for us. Come over here, please, Verne Hallam."

"You mean you ran into road agents?" Canby asked. He bowed to Nan and shook hands with Verne Hallam. Everyone was talking now, sharp inquiries rattling from all sides.

The two grim lawmen elbowed into the crowd. "Rufe says you were stuck up, Dan. Give us the lowdown."

"Happened at Indian Creek, Sheriff." Harbison gave a sketchy report and when he finished it the other lawman, whose badge revealed that he was a deputy United States marshal, began checking with the stage passengers. All five of them confirmed the driver's report. "But Verne Hallam here," Jim Agnew said, "is the only one who saw 'em unmasked. Verne, this is Marshal Orlando Robbins and he's poison to stage robbers. Tell him what you saw, boy."

While the baggage was being unloaded, Verne gave his story to the officers. Every eye was on him, there in the close-packed sidewalk crowd, so Verne saw something the others missed.

It was a deft and furtive movement of Lew

Rogan's right hand. Rogan had disembarked with the others, speaking to no-one except to give a nod of confirmation to Harbison's report.

Certainly he'd exchanged no word with Wade Canby. Yet now, in the close press, Verne saw Lew Rogan slip a folded note into Wade Canby's coat pocket. Then the man withdrew and stood apart from the others, paying no further attention to Canby.

The why of it puzzled Verne. According to the stage driver, Rogan was a shady dealer returning from a business trip to Salt Lake City. Why would he sneak a message to a reputable mining engineer who was soon to marry an attractive and well-to-do Boise City widow?

"Will you excuse us now, Sheriff?" Lois Lindsay asked, standing with a protective arm around Nan Stanley. "This poor child has been on the stage for fifty hours."

"Sure thing, Lois," Sheriff Oldham consented. "Harbison, come to my office and sign a report. Hallam, after supper you'd better drop up and make an affidavit about that forehead scar. Sounds like Floyd Plover. The two long skinny guys could be Frank Hugo and Dutch Schulte. Better go in now and get yourself a room."

Mrs. Lindsay led Nan into the Overland lobby and used her influence, which was considerable, to get the girl the best single room in the house. "Send her up some hot water right away, Amos.

Walter, you bring in her luggage. I'll be back at six to take her to supper. You too, Verne Hallam." With a smile at Verne she turned to her fiancé. "I need to freshen up myself, Wade, so you'd better take me home." She took Canby's arm and went out to the carriage he had waiting.

As they drove to her house on elm-lined Warm Springs Avenue, an odd preoccupation on her fiancé's face wasn't missed by Lois. It was the first time she'd ever known him to be inattentive. "Is anything wrong, Wade?"

"Wrong? Of course not." Canby reassembled his wits and tried to stop puzzling about the note Lew Rogan had slipped into his coat pocket.

It wasn't like Rogan. Rogan was discreet. When sent on some secret errand like the one which had taken him to Salt Lake City, he usually waited till Canby was alone in his office before reporting. Normally he would come slipping around late at night.

But this time something was so urgent that the man had sneaked a message to him right under the noses of two law officers. Canby itched to read it but naturally he couldn't in front of Lois.

Rogan's Salt Lake City errand had been quite simple. Six months ago a Salt Lake City man had inherited a shut-down Idaho mine of whose value he had no idea. By mail he'd employed Canby to appraise it. An examination had convinced Canby that the property was worth ten thousand dollars. But his report to the client appraised it as having only a speculative value of not more than fifteen hundred. After collecting his fee and waiting five months Canby had sent Rogan to Salt Lake City to pose as a speculator and offer two thousand for the mine. If the offer was accepted, Rogan would later reassign the title to Canby for half the eight-thousand-dollar profit.

Had the man suspected collusion between Canby and Rogan? If that was the burden of Rogan's surreptitious note, it still didn't make sense. A warning like that could wait till there was an opportunity to meet Canby privately.

"Tomorrow," Lois said, "I'm going down the valley to pick up Mark. Would you like to go with me?"

"Yes," the engineer said absently. Lois's nine-year-old son had gone to visit friends on a farm during his mother's absence at Rocky Bar.

"You're not very talkative," Lois chided. "I hope you're not displeased because I invited that nice boy and girl to have supper with us. She's lonely and a little frightened, I think. A supper date with a good-looking young man is just what she needs."

"I liked the cut of him myself," Canby said. "But if he's wise he won't hang around too long. Floyd Plover's got more than one back-alley heeler here in town."

"That's what Lew Rogan said at Dunn's station."

Mention of Rogan again fixed Canby's mind on the note in his pocket. He drove on down the avenue under an arch of stately elms, past handsome Victorian residences unmatched anywhere else in Idaho Territory. A score of men who'd garnered fortunes during the Sixties when gold had flowed freely from the gravel beds around Idaho City had built imposing mansions on this street.

Lois Lindsay's house was comparatively modest. Although the half-acre lawn had a fountain and a cast iron deer, the house itself was not much larger than its owner needed for herself, her growing son and her Swedish maid. Wade Canby turned into the driveway and stopped at the well-scrubbed front steps.

The door opened and Helga, the rawboned Scandinavian who'd served Lois since the infancy of Marcus, Jr., stood there with a welcoming smile.

"We're going right back to town as soon as I change, Helga," Lois said as they went in. "Wade, if you'll wait in the parlor Helga will bring you a glass of sherry."

Lois hurried upstairs and Canby went into the formal parlor. The instant Helga withdrew he took Rogan's note from his pocket and began reading it:

Here's something that won't wait. She's no widow. Two days ago I saw Marcus Lindsay alive at Kelton. Must have been somebody else they dug out from under that pile of rock, back in '69 . . .

To Canby it was incredible. Was Rogan tricking him? There was more to the note but the return of Helga with a tray made Canby slip it back into his pocket. True or not, its very existence was dynamite. Lois, he knew, would promptly cancel her engagement to him on any mere whisper that Marcus Lindsay might be alive. For ten years she and all of Idaho had believed him dead.

Canby took sherry from the tray and waited for the servant to leave the room. But flowers in a vase needed rearranging and Helga took a minute or two for it. While she was at it Canby's mind flashed back to the known facts of the mine explosion ten years ago in Squaw Creek Canyon.

The accidental setting off of a box of dynamite had not only buried the miner under tons of rock, mangling him, but the blast had burned the very skin from his face. The corpse they'd dug out of the debris would have been unidentifiable except that it wore Lindsay's leather coat—that and the fact that Lindsay was known to be working the test tunnel alone. Who else could it have been but Marcus Lindsay?

Lois herself had never doubted it. Especially as

the years passed without Lindsay ever being seen or heard of again.

At last Helga left the room and Canby could finish reading the note:

You wouldn't know him to look at him. His face and head are disfigured by old burns and powder pits. Calls himself John Gresham. He's bearded at the chin, fire-scarred everywhere above the beard. He's left-handed and blue-eyed and so was Lindsay. When we came face to face at Kelton he seemed to recognize me. And his voice is Lindsay's. He'd just applied for a stage driving job at the Wells Fargo office in Kelton. They turned him down, maybe on account of his looks. But I happen to know that Wells Fargo always makes an applicant fill out a form telling about his past and even giving the date of his birth. So I went into the Kelton Wells Fargo office and asked to see the form John Gresham had just filled out. It said he'd been a wagoneer for the past nine years in California and Arizona. It gave his birth date as November 24, 1839. Naturally he'd give a false name but he might automatically write down his true birth date. If I was you I'd look it up, P.D.Q.

To Canby it was still unbelievable. In any case he was determined not to let it interfere with his marriage to Lois. For one thing she was the most desirable woman he'd ever known. For another he desperately needed her fortune. Certain schemes had gone awry and he had heavy, overdue debts.

His eyes swept the parlor and fixed on a leather-bound book on a corner table. It was the family Bible which Lois had brought with her from Virginia long ago. Certain vital statistics should be recorded there. Canby went to it and opened it to a fly-leaf page used for keeping the family record.

The birth, marriage and death dates of Lois's parents were there. Under these the record said:

Daughter, LOIS, born August 4, 1846, at Roanoke, Virginia. Married June 28, 1867, to MARCUS LINDSAY at Boise City, Idaho. MARCUS LINDSAY, born Nov. 24, 1839; died May 23, 1869. Son, MARCUS, Jr., born at Boise City, Dec. 8, 1869. . . .

Wade Canby stared dismally at that date: Nov. 24, 1839. It could hardly be a coincidence. Why would the man at Kelton have used that date unless he was really Marcus Lindsay?

CHAPTER III

Verne, in his room at the Overland, shaved and put on a fresh shirt. He brushed his wavy, reddish hair and polished his boots. He couldn't do more, because most of his belongings were in a trail pack which wouldn't arrive till tomorrow. At six o'clock he went down to the lobby and found it crowded with trailsmen, uniformed officers from Fort Boise and townspeople about to take supper here. The lobby had a cigar counter in one corner, while across from it, with a wicker cage like a bank teller's, was the local Wells Fargo office. Ten years ago Lois Lindsay had clerked there. How warm and friendly she was, Verne thought, inviting two young strangers to have supper with her!

The Overland's host, Charlie Eastman, came up heartily. "A mighty neat show you put on down the road, boy! The town's buzzin' about it. They're bad actors, that Plover gang. Come into the bar and I'll buy you a drink."

"No thanks. It'd spoil my supper." Verne didn't bother to say that in all his twenty-one years he'd never tasted anything stronger than coffee.

"Speaking of supper," the hotel man said, "I reserved a table for Lois Lindsay. There's a woman for you! Mighty lucky guy, that Wade Canby is."

Verne barely heard him, for his eyes were on Nan Stanley as she came down the stairs. She'd changed into a blue dinner dress whose bell-shaped skirt had three tiers of ruffles. As she reached the foot of the steps Verne was waiting there. His eyes and his impulsive words said the same thing. "You look mighty pretty, Nan."

A man's voice spoke behind him. "I was about to say the same thing, Hallam."

Wade Canby was standing there with Mrs. Lindsay. The two had just entered from the street.

"And I, too," Lois echoed. "Shall we go in?"

With Canby she led the way and Nan followed, her hand lightly on Verne's arm. A lobbyful of onlookers watched their progress to the dining room and Verne heard a whisky *sotto* in the background: "Lois always does the right thing, and she can pick a thoroughbred every time."

"Which do you mean, Ed? The cowboy or the gal?"

"Both."

The Overland's head waitress came up. "I got your message, Mrs. Lindsay. This way, please." She led them to a table set for four. The hotel's finest linen and silver were on it together with a vase of fresh roses.

"You make me feel like I'm really important," Nan said to her hostess.

"But you are," the older woman insisted earnestly. "You're bringing youth and gentleness and beauty to a hard, rough land. Idaho needs you a good deal more than you need Idaho."

When they were seated Wade Canby raised a hand to salute a group across the room. In a lowered voice he identified them to Verne Hallam. "The man with the beard is Governor Biggerstaff. The two with him are Milt Kelly, editor of the *Statesman*, and John Hailey, who owns the stage line you came in on."

The supper had been ordered in advance and the courses came smoothly. Proprietor Eastman came up, deferentially, to make sure everything was right. "Why didn't you bring the boy along, Lois?"

"He's having fun on a farm," Lois said. "I'm going after him tomorrow."

Other prominent people stopped to pay their respects. To Verne it became clear that Mrs. Lindsay ranked at the very top of the social ladder here in the Idaho capital. The commandant at Fort Boise stopped for a word of greeting. Nan smiled shyly and Verne stood up to shake hands. "We're having a ball at the post a week from Thursday," the colonel announced, "and I'm inviting you young folks right now."

"Thank you," Nan said.

"And you, Verne Hallam?" Lois Lindsay questioned. "You'll be here that long, won't you?"

Verne looked straight at Nan. "I hadn't planned to. But I've just changed my mind."

There was oyster soup, prairie chicken salad, leg of lamb, chocolate cake and French coffee. During the dessert course Wade Canby asked Nan: "I hear your brothers are bringing some cattle from Kelton. How many drovers have they got?"

"None, other than themselves," the girl told him. "But they've got a covered wagon, too. So in Kelton they hired a man to drive it. It was just before I left there on the stage."

"I hope he's trustworthy," Canby said. "Lots of tough characters around Kelton."

"I didn't see the man," Nan said. "But I heard my brother Paul mention his name. Gresham, I believe. John Gresham."

The spoon fell from Wade Canby's hand and clattered on the floor. A strained look on his face made Lois ask: "Aren't you feeling well, Wade?"

"Must've choked on something," Canby murmured. Before he could say more a band began playing noisily just beyond an open window.

"It's the Capital Brass Band," Lois explained. "It always serenades the governor when he dines here.—Ah, good evening, Doctor. I want you to know my friends, Nan Stanley and Verne Hallam. This is Doctor Eph Smith." Again Verne stood up to shake hands.

"The county owes you a medal, young man." Eph Smith smiled at Nan and passed on.

When supper was over Lois took her guests to

the hotel parlor, where others came in to meet them. For the next hour it was like a reception— merchants, bankers, mine owners, army officers in uniform going in and out.

At nine Mrs. Lindsay broke it up. "This girl has been riding a stage coach for two days and nights. It's time you were in bed, Nan."

Verne took Nan to the stairs and then went out to their carriage with his hostess and Wade Canby. After seeing them off he remembered the sheriff's instruction to sign a statement describing the three highwaymen.

The jail was only a block up Eighth Street and he found Sheriff Oldham at his desk.

"The posse's already on its way," Oldham said. "Chances are those buggers'll foul their sign in creek water. But one of 'em's got a bloody arm. It can slow him up. Or he could stop somewhere to have it patched. Depends on how bad you nicked him."

When Verne finished writing his statement the sheriff called in a notary to witness the signing of it.

"Want to see the sights, Hallam?" the notary asked. "Too early to go to bed. We can take a walk down Idaho Street, if you feel like it."

"What's there to see down Idaho Street?"

"Saloon Row, the red light line, the Bonanza gambling house, couple of variety shows and Chinatown. Almost anything you want."

"All I want right now," Verne grinned, "is a soft bed and ten hours sleep."

Twenty minutes later he was asleep in his room at the Overland. The sharp rapping at his door seemed to come almost at once. But when he got up and lighted a lamp Verne's watch told him that it was three in the morning.

"What is it?"

"You're wanted at Doc Smith's," a voice beyond the door answered.

Dressing hurriedly, Verne remembered meeting Doctor Eph Smith at supper. He unlocked the door and let the messenger in.

He was a chunky, middle-aged man out of breath from running. "I'm Bob Baker," the man announced. "A guy with a fresh bullet hole through his arm just routed Eph Smith out of bed. Said he was cleanin' his gun and it went off accidental. Wound's in bad shape and it'll fester if it's not treated right away. Eph thinks he's on the level but he wants to make sure."

"Why didn't he call in a constable?"

Baker shrugged. "He'd look silly, having a patient arrested if the guy's on the level. Anyway, he says you're the only one who can give a yes or no on it."

That was true. Only Verne had seen the three unmasked faces. "Is the guy heeled with a gun?"

"Nope. That's one reason why Eph Smith

figgers he ain't one of the stage robbers. It's only a few blocks from here."

They hurried downstairs and out to the street. It was dark except for saloon lights. Baker led the way down Main to Sixth and there turned south to Grove Street.

Grove Street was lined with residences and quite dark. Half a block east from Sixth they came to a picket gate with a shingle over it. In the dim night light Verne made out a name: EPHRAIM SMITH, M.D.

Beyond the gate a clapboard house had a lamp glow at one of its windows. Baker went only as far as the front door. "The Doc says for you to go right in. He's stallin' till you get there, Hallam. He pretended to be out of iodine and stepped out to get some. I was passin' by and he flagged me down. All he wants is for you to take a look at the guy. If he's not one of the road agents, you're to say you've got a sore back and need some pain pills. You take 'em and get right out."

Verne nodded. The house door wasn't locked. He opened it and stepped into a lamplit hallway. At once the bareness of the hall told him he'd been tricked. This was an empty house and he'd been decoyed to it by the man calling himself Baker. It wouldn't have been hard to steal the doctor's shingle from another gate farther down the street.

Before Verne could retreat, doors on either

side of the hall opened and two men came at him from opposite directions. As Verne pulled the gun from his holster, one of the men smashed an iron pipe down on his head. The second man grabbed his wrist and for half a minute Verne Hallam, staggering dizzily, struggled with his assailant for possession of the gun. The first man hit him again with the pipe and Verne went to his knees, still clutching the grip of his gun. As the second man twisted his wrist to make him drop it, Verne squeezed the trigger and sent a shot upward. Plaster sprinkled down from the ceiling while the man with the pipe kept pounding him on the head.

Neither of these men, Verne knew from his brief glimpse of their faces, was any of the three who'd held up Harbison's stage. His last awareness was of a shrill whistle from down Grove Street and the sound of steps running fast toward the house.

"Jigger!" the man with the pipe warned. "It's the night constable. He must've heard the shot." Twice again the man struck hard with the pipe and Verne lay stunned and bleeding on the hall floor.

CHAPTER IV

All day Wade Canby waited in his office, fretfully impatient to see Rogan. The office was upstairs in Broadbent's stone block at Sixth and Main, better known as the "Stone Jug," with the Palace restaurant, Jauman's bar and Coffin's hardware store on the ground floor. Except for Canby's office, the upper floor was occupied entirely by lawyers. Governor Biggerstaff himself had an office here, while the Honorable Tom Curtis, Probate Judge of Ada County, had a suite at the west end of the hall. Huston and Gray had the east suite and Canby's smaller office was at the center, directly at the head of the Main Street stairs.

All day clients of one office or another clattered up and down those stairs. No doubt Lew Rogan was aware of it and would keep away until after dark.

Yet so impatient was Canby to see the man that he'd begged off from a drive with Lois Lindsay, after promising he'd go with her. She was bringing her boy back from the valley farm. "Just got word an important client from Silver City's coming to see me," had been Canby's excuse after seeing Lois home from the Overland the night before.

45

He might as well have gone along, for when evening came Rogan still hadn't put in an appearance. Canby took supper at the Central Hotel where he kept a permanent room. For economy's sake he'd moved there from the Overland when a bad investment had stripped him almost to his last dollar. He owed a sizable note at the First National Bank of Idaho and John Huntoon, the cashier, would probably have cracked down on him already except that he knew Wade Canby was soon to marry a well-to-do widow who herself was a director of the bank.

During supper Canby heard a buzz of talk about a cowboy who'd been decoyed to an empty house just before daybreak and clubbed senseless there. It didn't greatly interest him. He went up to his room, planning a return to his office when it was quite dark.

But just as the light was fading his door opened and Lew Rogan slipped furtively in. The man's coming to his hotel room angered Canby. He'd given strict orders against it. He didn't want this pussy-footing fixer to be seen inquiring for him at the lobby desk.

"It's all right," Rogan assured him with a wink. "I registered myself and took a room down the hall. Nobody seen me come in your room."

Canby looked out to see if the hall was empty, closed a window, then spoke in a guarded voice. "Let's have the straight of it, Lew."

46

Rogan hitched his chair nearer. Sitting knee to knee with Canby he gave a report which repeated and amplified the note he'd slipped into Canby's coat pocket.

"I figure he's Mark Lindsay, all right. If you think back you'll recollect they was only three reasons for identifyin' the body as Lindsay's. It had on Lindsay's leather coat; Lindsay had been workin' alone in the tunnel; and he was never seen again alive or dead."

Savagely Canby bit off the end of a cigar, and sat chewing it and glaring bitterly into space. "I wouldn't believe it," he said, "except for the birth date. He put it down exactly right on that Wells Fargo form. Nobody would know it except Lindsay himself."

"You asked his wife?"

"Of course not, stupid. But I looked it up and it's right."

"Kinda puts you in a box, don't it? You can't very well marry a married woman."

"That part of it's all right," Canby said. "Legally she's a widow. There's a law that says when a husband disappears and is presumed to be dead for more than seven years, and in all that time is never heard from, his wife may consider herself a widow and remarry without bigamy."

Relief showed on Rogan's fleshy, unshaven face. "Then there ain't nothin' to worry about."

"There's everything to worry about," Canby

47

snapped. "If Lois finds out he's alive she'll stick with him and give me the gate."

"Not if she sees what he looks like," Rogan argued. "He's a shade uglier'n a mud fence. You ain't got no idea what that powder blast done to his face."

"It wouldn't make any difference to Lois." She'd loved her husband, Canby well knew. He was equally sure that Lois had consented to marry himself partly out of loneliness and partly because her boy had reached an age when he needed the companionship of a father. He, Canby, would instantly become second choice to the real father, no matter how disfigured the man's face.

"You haven't heard the worst of it," Canby confided darkly. "After the Wells Fargo people turned down his application at Kelton, he got on as a teamster for a trail outfit heading for Boise City—two brothers named Stanley with a wagon and three hundred cows."

"I heard about 'em," Rogan said. "The Stanley girl rode up on the stage with me. But she didn't say nothin' about her menfolks hirin' a teamster."

"She did at supper last night. Said his name's John Gresham. Means he'll be here in about three weeks."

"The devil you say! You reckon he aims to walk in on his wife?"

The engineer shook his head moodily. "He's not

that kind, Lew. When I knew him Mark Lindsay was about as decent and unselfish a man as you could find. I don't know how he got out of that mine cave-in but apparently he did. Somebody must've hauled him away and taken care of him for a while. No telling who or how or why. Maybe by the time he was able to think things out he learned he was supposed to be dead and buried. He might figure he'd be a burden and an eyesore to his wife if he went back to her. He'd think of what was best for her, not what was best for himself."

"But later he got well enough to hold down teamster jobs," Rogan said. "According to the form he filled out for Wells Fargo, he worked nine years at it all through California and Arizona."

"No telling what was in his mind," Canby brooded. "Chances are he didn't know he had a son. He could've heard about it for the first time in Utah only a month or so ago. A boy nine and a half years old with the name Marcus, Jr., would be his own son. He'd want to see him and he'd want to see Lois. That could be why he hired out as a teamster to Boise City."

"You mean he'd come all the way here just for a look at 'em, without tellin' 'em who he is?"

"I can't think of any other reason, Lew. If he's kept out of his wife's life for ten years he wouldn't be likely to come into it now. If she sees him only at a distance she won't know him. You

49

say he's all fire-scarred and powder-pitted from the beard up?"

"He sure is," Rogan confirmed. "But he's still got Lindsay's voice and blue eyes. If he stays here long enough, somebody'll get the same hunch I got and tip off his wife."

"The worst of it," Canby worried, "is that he's working for the Stanley brothers and Lois has sort of taken the Stanley girl under her wing. It might bring 'em all together, somehow. It shapes up bad, Lew. You rode the stage with that girl. What else did she say about her brothers?"

"To me nothing. But she talked a good deal to Jim Agnew and Mrs. Lindsay. Said the Stanley boys aim to buy or lease a small ranch somewhere in the Boise Valley. They're bringing along stock for it and a bank draft for five thousand dollars."

"Five thousand dollars," Canby pondered, "would be pretty good road-agent bait if it was in cash instead of a bank draft."

Rogan squinted at him curiously. "Meanin' what?"

"Meaning I'm assigning you a new job." Canby's eyes narrowed and his tone had hard edges. "It's to see that Mark Lindsay never gets here."

Rogan quickly backed away from it. "Not me. I'm no drygulcher. If you figure to have me lay low by the trail and pick that teamster off . . ."

"You won't need to get within fifty miles of him," Canby broke in. "In fact you won't even have to leave town. You heard what happened to that cowboy Hallam last night, didn't you?"

"Sure. They're gassin' about it at every bar up the street. He got the hell beat out of him by some pals of the Plover gang."

"How's he doing? Did you hear?"

"They moved him a few doors down Grove Street to Doc Smith's house and Eph put him to bed there. Says he'll be laid up for a week maybe. Coupla more licks and them guys would've chonked his brains out. Constable Paxton happened to be walkin' the Grove Street beat and he heard a gunshot in the empty house. He got there in time to scare 'em off."

"It proves one thing for certain," Canby concluded. "The Plover gang has close connections here in town. Got any idea who they are?"

"Nothin' anybody could prove," Rogan said. "But the wise word along Idaho Street is that the gang's listening post is Baldy Smeed's bar on Fifth just off China Alley. The night bartender there's a gink name Dutch Henry and I've heard he's Floyd Plover's brother-in-law, although he won't admit it. This Dutch Henry once served a term for passin' bogus gold dust at Placerville, back in '67."

"How well do you know him?"

Rogan shrugged. "Well enough to take a drink

51

at his bar now and then. Why shouldn't I? It's a licensed saloon, ain't it?"

"Take another drink there tonight, Lew. And listen!" Canby leaned forward and in a hushed voice gave his agent one final, concise instruction.

To carry it out Rogan waited till nearly midnight before going into a shabby bar where China Alley opened into Fifth Street. It was a smelly place with sawdust on the floor. Bad whisky was a bit per drink and beer was a dime a schooner. There were no games, no women, no piano, no free lunch, nothing but cheap drinks and coarse customers and a fat bartender named Dutch Henry.

"Draw one, Dutch," Rogan said.

Dutch Henry filled a schooner and slid it across the bar. Other customers were there. One of them knew Rogan by sight and the inevitable question came. "I hear you was in that stage that got stuck up, Rogan, down at Indian Crik. What about it?"

The same remark had been made to Lew Rogan in every public place he'd entered since arriving on the stage. He'd counted on it being made here and it was just the cue he needed.

"Yep," he said. "It like to scared me to death, too. But not half as much as it scared that Stanley gal. She's just a tenderfoot kid and a long way from home. Figures to wait here for a couple of big brothers who're headin' this way from Kelton with the makings of a cow ranch."

Rogan now had the full attention of everyone at the bar, including the bartender himself. His thought was that any really important information he gave out to the bartender would in the end reach the man's outlaw brother-in-law, Floyd Plover. He knew too that the Plover gang weren't cattle thieves, although they might steal a good horse now and then.

"You mean they're comin' here with a cattle herd?"

"Yep, and five thousand in cash to buy land with," Lew said. "That's the kinda folks we need in this country. Folks with stock and capital, not just busted immigrants like most of these covered-wagon people are. Fill her up again, Dutch."

Dutch Henry replenished the schooner, then leaned across the bar with a cocked eye. "How big a trail outfit have they got, these Stanley boys?"

"Just the two of 'em," Rogan said, "and some tramp they picked up at Kelton to drive the wagon for 'em."

"When did they leave Kelton?"

"They're leavin' there right now. Take 'em maybe three weeks to get here."

Looking slyly over his beer Rogan could see that Dutch Henry was impressed. Actually he'd told the truth except in one detail. The money was in a bank draft instead of in cash. But cash would be the word to set off Floyd Plover. To get it, would he bushwhack the Stanley drive? If he did there'd be a fight—a gunfight in which the Stanley brothers and their wagoneer were likely to be outnumbered and sure to be outgunned. They might even be wiped out.

CHAPTER V

On the second day north out of Kelton the Stanley outfit crossed from Utah into the Idaho Territory. Only a pile of rocks marked the line. Marcus Lindsay, driving a mule-drawn wagon, scanned the horizon ahead but could see nothing to suggest a waterhole. The cattle were a mile behind him and he'd been told to make camp at the first water.

The wagon was bumping along over virgin sod. The stage road to Boise City and Oregon lay well to the left of them but by keeping wide of it they could find better grass. Paul and Warren Stanley were wise and patient drovers.

Twice today the wagoneer had come to an arroyo which he couldn't cross with wheels. Each time he'd detoured to the main trail, to a crossing used by freighters and stagecoaches. But as nearly as possible he kept directly in advance of the cattle.

Three hundred head weren't too many for the brothers to handle as long as they didn't need to worry about the wagon. The wagoneer also did most of the cooking and camp making. The three made a good crew and now Marcus Lindsay was glad he'd failed to get the Wells Fargo job.

The cattle were mostly two-year-old heifers,

Utah-bred, and looking back, Lindsay could see their dust. Grass was thin along here and the Stanleys were pushing the stock a little. On good feed they moved much slower. Lindsay veered his team to keep a wheel from hitting a rock. The wagon was loaded mainly with essential items of household goods selected from the old Stanley home in Ohio and shipped by rail to Kelton.

The brothers had been kind to him and Lindsay liked them. By now he knew that they had a young sister who'd gone ahead by stage. He'd missed seeing her at Kelton. Nor had the girl seen him. Women rarely looked at Marcus Lindsay and the few who did were likely to show either pity or revulsion, or to look quickly away. Lindsay was used to it. For ten years it had been like that.

And now here he was heading back toward the one place he'd sworn never to show himself again. Not that there was one chance in a hundred that anyone there would recognize him. How could they, after ten years, with his fire-scarred face and forehead and hairless head, and with his lower face bushily bearded? In the old days he'd been clean-cut and beardless. He'd left Idaho at the age of thirty and now, though only forty, he looked nearer sixty. At Kelton he'd run into several freighters and stage line hands he'd known ten years ago in Idaho, and not one of them had recognized him.

At Boise City he'd keep in the background and from a distance perhaps catch a few glimpses of Lois and the boy. Life at least owed him that much. He hadn't even known about the boy until a month ago when a teaming job had landed him in Salt Lake City. The social page in a Sunday paper there had announced the engagement of a popular Boise City widow to a mining engineer named Wade Canby. The bride-to-be, it said, was Mrs. Lois Lindsay, mother of a nine-year-old son, Marcus, Jr.

Ahead on the prairie Lindsay could see a clump of stunted cottonwoods and knew he'd find water there. It was sundown and time to make camp. The grade was slightly downward and he coaxed the mules to an easy trot.

At the cottonwoods he found a wash with a thin trickle in it. Here and there a pool in the bed would furnish overnight stock water. It was only the eighth day of June. Later in the summer this semi-desert wash would be dry.

Lindsay drew up under shade and unhitched there. He staked the mules out in the best grass he could find. Then he unloaded a camp kit and made a fire. All the while the cattle drive came nearer, the heifers lowing at the smell of water.

Around a supper fire under starlight, Paul and Warren Stanley talked buoyantly of the new life awaiting them in Idaho. Paul was twenty-six and Warren a year older. It was the second trail supper and their camaraderie heartened Marcus Lindsay. They no longer seemed to notice his disfigurements and were treating him like one of the family.

"You're a darn good cook, John," Paul said. They knew him only as John Gresham.

"And you can sure handle a wagon," Warren added. "How'd you like to work for us permanently? Paul and I'll have more'n we can handle, starting a cow ranch on a strange range."

"Not to mention," Paul said, "filing a couple of homesteads and proving up on 'em."

"Homesteads?" the wagoneer asked. "Thought you said you aim to buy or lease a ready-made layout?"

"We've got a bank draft for five thousand dollars to do just that," Paul Stanley explained. "We'll probably lease with an option to buy. If we buy we'll put the title in Nan's name. Nan's our kid sister. But she's only nineteen and can't file on land herself. Warren and I can, provided we're legally landless. So we figure to take out a couple of homesteads adjoining whatever ranch we buy or lease. After we prove up, it'll fatten our fence lines just that much."

"A lot of big western ranches were built up like that," Warren put in. "You start with a core of deeded land and then fatten it with government filings on both sides."

"What about it, John?" Paul prodded. "We can keep you right on the payroll, if you like, and you could help us get settled on a ranch."

"I'm no hand with cattle," Lindsay told them. "All I know is horses and mules and wagons."

"Paul and I could handle the cattle," Warren argued, "if we had a good extra hand like you to take care of the chores and do the driving and general handy work. Think it over, John."

The man with the disfigured face *did* think it over as he lay in his blankets that night. He considered it wistfully and was tempted. For ten years he'd had no family or people or anyone to share a home with. It would be good to feel once more that he belonged somewhere and was wanted, and could end an existence of aimless wandering, driving over desert and mountain for first one freight line and then another.

He wanted to grow roots again, but did he dare do it near Boise City? If he did, sooner or later he'd come face to face with Lois. If she heard his voice, or noticed some old familiar gesture, she might know him. It would be a frightful shock to her after all these years. It would turn the clock back and shatter the new life she'd made for herself. She was the kind to insist on taking him back and that, Mark Lindsay had irrevocably decided, wouldn't be fair to either Lois or the boy.

Best if he only hung around the Boise basin

long enough for a few glimpses of them. Then he could move on again, to California or Oregon or Montana, burying himself as effectively as the real John Gresham lay buried under a headstone bearing the name Marcus Lindsay.

He could never forget those last few days of his old life, ten years ago in Squaw Creek Canyon. He'd been working alone there and everyone knew it, driving a test tunnel and using dynamite to blast rock. Along had come a tramp miner, down-and-out and hungry, and Lindsay had put him up in his sod shack, fed him, loaned him a warm leather coat, and hired him at day pay to speed work in the tunnel. An expert with explosives, John Gresham like many miners was inclined to be careless with them. He was likely to crimp a cap with his teeth and to take other chances.

On that last tragic day Marcus Lindsay had just wheeled a barrow load of tailings out of the tunnel to a dump heap. While he was gone John Gresham, who had just drilled a blast hole into the heading, had crimped a cap over a fuse and pressed it into the end of a dynamite stick. Normally he would push the stick into the blast hole, tamp around and over it, then light the protruding fuse and hurry out of the tunnel to await the explosion. Lindsay, who'd already gone out with a wheelbarrow, was presumably in the clear.

Marcus Lindsay couldn't be sure just what

had happened. His guess was that Gresham had found his blast hole not quite deep enough to accommodate the charge. Perhaps he'd removed the charge, already capped, and laid it on a box behind him from which the stick of dynamite had just been taken. In that case Gresham would pick up a drill and hand sledge, insert the drill into the hole and pound the sledge on it to make the hole a bit deeper.

When it was deep enough he might toss the drill and sledge aside in order to re-insert the capped charge into the hole. Before lighting the fuse his intention would be to carry the dynamite box out of the tunnel. But if the tossed sledge hammer happened to land on the capped charge the impact would detonate the cap, which would detonate the charge, which in turn would detonate the entire box of explosives.

In some such way it might have happened. Lindsay knew only that he himself was wheeling the empty barrow back into the tunnel when the explosion came. The blast of it had burned the skin of his face and forehead and the hair from the top of his head. It had blown him bodily out of the tunnel. Gresham, much nearer the heading, had been unrecognizably mangled and buried under tons of rock.

Except for the blinding flash, Marcus Lindsay remembered nothing of the explosion. It was a week before he'd known anything at all. His first awareness was that he was lying on deerskins in the teepee of Sam Longfish. A year earlier Sam Longfish had been captured by vigilantes and accused of stealing a horse. They were about to shoot him when Marcus Lindsay had come along and stopped it, forcing the vigilantes to turn Sam over to the law at Idaho City. While the Indian was in jail awaiting trial his innocence was proved by the capture of the real horse thief near Placerville.

It was a year later that Lindsay lay in the Longfish lodge hovering between life and death. The Indian, finding him outside the tunnel stunned, burned and apparently blinded for life, had laid him across a horse and brought him there. Sam's squaw and his elderly father who'd been a tribal medicine man, had given what first aid they could. When he was able to think he realized that by now the mine disaster would have been discovered and investigated. They would have taken what was left of John Gresham out from under tons of rock—a mangled body wearing Lindsay's leather coat! Would they think it was Lindsay himself?

To find out he'd sent Sam Longfish down to Middleton, a stage station on the Overland Road, to listen in on gossip there. Sam's report was that the mine casualty had been identified as Marcus Lindsay and buried by the widow, Lois, at Boise City.

A burning pain at his eyes had given Lindsay a foreboding of permanent blindness. That, and his disfigured face, had made him shrink from appearing before Lois to become a burden for the rest of his life. Since she thought he was dead and buried, it was better that she keep on thinking so.

After another despondent week Marcus Lindsay had figured a way out of it. He knew of a covered wagon family stranded alongside the Overland Trail, their money gone and their wagon team stolen by outlaw raiders. The Seebrees from Missouri had been on their way to Oregon with two small children. The woman, who was expecting another baby, had a cousin in Oregon who might give them shelter if they could get there.

"Take me to them," Lindsay had said to Sam Longfish. And when the Indian had carted him there Lindsay had made a proposition to Jed Seebree. "I have enough money in my wallet to buy a good team and pay travelling expenses to Umatilla. It's yours if you'll take me along in your covered wagon."

The name he gave was Gresham and the Seebrees had no idea who he really was. They were a month on the way to Umatilla, Oregon, where a doctor had treated Lindsay's eyes and given him hope that in time he might regain nearly normal vision. His face, forehead and scalp would always be blackened in spots, scarred and powder-pitted in others.

Slowly he'd regained strength and a day came when he was able to hire out as a teamster. He grew a beard to cover the disfigurements on the lower half of his face, but above the beard his skin seemed to become more hideous than ever. More and more he shrank from resurrecting himself as Marcus Lindsay. Lois, at Boise City, considered herself a widow and was making a new life.

Just how prosperous a life that was Lindsay didn't learn until recently when he'd read about her in a Salt Lake City paper. The news story of her coming marriage to Wade Canby briefly reviewed her rise from a Wells Fargo ticket clerk to a position at the very top of the Idaho capital's social, banking and mining circles. She and her nine-year-old son, Marcus, lived on fashionable Warm Springs Avenue. All the elite of Ada County would attend her marriage there.

The boy, Lindsay knew at once, could only be his own son.

As for the husband-to-be, Lindsay remembered him as an enterprising engineer in the old days at Idaho City. A man distinctly personable and as far as Lindsay knew of excellent professional standing. What a shadow of contrast would be cast if he, Marcus Lindsay, should present himself there!

A look or two at Lois and the boy was all that he could decently hope for. He'd checked the legalities of the matter and knew that legally Lois was a widow and could remarry without bigamy, because of the seven-year statute of limitations on husbands presumed to be dead that long.

Over and over Marcus Lindsay thought of these things as he lay in his blankets under the Stanley wagon, two nights north out of Kelton.

He was up early to get a fire going. Dried stalks of black sage made fuel for him. "Today we'll tie the remounts to your endgate, John," Paul decided over coffee. "Loose horses don't handle very well on a cattle drive."

The outfit only had four saddle horses and the Stanleys had been changing from mount to mount twice a day. The three hundred young cows, after bedding down for the night near the waterhole, had been grazing since daybreak. "We'll let 'em feed an hour longer," Warren said. "You go ahead any time you're ready, John."

After graining the mules Lindsay used lead ropes to tie the remounts to his endgate. When he climbed to the driver's seat he had Paul's double-barreled shotgun beside him. The outfit needed fresh meat and today he'd keep on a lookout for prairie chickens.

During the morning his creaking wagon flushed several of them and once, as a pair whirred off, the sound frightened his mules into a near runaway.

Would they be gunshy, Lindsay wondered, if he had to shoot from the wagon seat?

In the afternoon he saw a few buffalo on the horizon and a small band of antelope came within rifle shot of his wagon. But Lindsay had only a shotgun.

That day the drive made almost fifteen miles and still kept well to the right of the stage road. But on the fourth day of the trek a rocky ridge forced Lindsay to veer left and just before camping time he struck the Kelton-Boise City stage road on the bank of Raft Creek. It was shadeless except for an occasional flat bend where a few cottonwoods grew.

When Lindsay chose one of these for a night stop he found a man with a small, canvas-covered sheep wagon already camped there. "Make yourself at home, podner," the man said with a friendly grin. "This here's a lonesome country and I don't mind company."

His name was Jess Younger and he had a sheep ranch west of Raft Creek. He'd been out after meat and today had shot a buffalo and half a dozen sage hens. "More meat than I can eat, podner. Help yourself."

"Here comes my outfit," Lindsay said as the dust of the Stanley drive came in sight.

Younger pointed in the opposite direction. "And there comes a freight wagon. A bull outfit. Looks like an ore load headin' for Kelton."

The ore wagon had six yoke of oxen and its driver made camp down the creek a little way. "Silver ore from the Rocky Bar mines, likely," Younger guessed. "There ain't no smelter at Rocky Bar yet and they have to freight the ore to Kelton and then ship it by rail to Salt Lake. Takes most of the profit out of it. While you unhitch, podner, I'll go invite that bullwhacker to eat supper with us."

The Stanley drive came up and the heifers scattered to feed along Raft Creek. Lindsay picketed the mules and the remounts. "It's a hunter," he explained, thumbing toward the Younger wagon. "We've got a sage-hen supper coming up—him, us and a bullwhacker."

The friendly Jess Younger rejoined them. "He'll be with us soon as he unyokes, podners. Turns out he's an old friend of mine who used to drive a stage between Idaho City and Boise. Abe Earnshaw's his name. Any of you gents know him?"

The Stanleys, new to Idaho, didn't. But to Lindsay the name brought a startled apprehension. In his old life more than ten years ago he'd often ridden the stage between Idaho City and Boise and more than once had chatted with its driver, Abe Earnshaw.

Would the man know him? If he did, others at Boise City would also know him and the masquerade of John Gresham would be exposed.

Lindsay's first impulse was to take a walk up the creek on some pretext and stay out of sight until after dark. Later, with only the light of a campfire, Earnshaw would be less likely to recognize him.

Then Marcus Lindsay steeled himself for a test. He'd face the man and dare recognition. If Earnshaw recognized him he'd quit the Stanley outfit at the first opportunity and turn back alone to Kelton. But if the man failed to know him, he'd continue on with confidence to the Boise Basin and perhaps even accept permanent employment with the Stanleys.

CHAPTER VI

Twice during the sage-hen supper Lindsay saw the bullwhacker cock a curious eye his way. Both times it was right after Lindsay had spoken at length and he realized that the risk of recognition lay not in his face but in his voice.

After that he let the others do the talking.

It was brisk talk and the spark that fired it was the name Stanley.

"You boys any kin to that gal who was in the Indian Crik hold-up last week?" Earnshaw inquired. "Nan Stanley, they say her name was."

It was the first Paul and Warren had heard of Nan's mishap. They bombarded the bullwhacker with questions.

"She didn't get hurt none," he assured them. "I wouldn't know about it myself if I hadn't stopped for coffee at a relay station day before yesterday. The coach headin' this way changed horses there and the driver gave me the lowdown on it. The Plover gang, he said. Three of 'em, all masked. Cowboy by the name of Hallam came along and driv 'em off. Coupla ladies was aboard. Your sister and Lois Lindsay from Boise. A mighty fine woman, Lois is. Knew her when she usta clerk for Wells Fargo."

"You're sure they weren't hurt?" Paul asked.

69

"Not a scratch. Didn't get robbed, neither, thanks to that cowboy Hallam. Somebody beat Hallam up, though, the next night in town. Sheriff's got a posse out lookin' for the Plover gang but it ain't had no luck yet."

The genial Jess Younger passed a platter. "And help yourself to some more coffee, podners. Who else was on that stage? Anybody I know?"

"Jim Agnew was on it. And a drummer from Denver. And Lew Rogan. Remember Lew? Back in the Sixties he usta be a constable at Idaho City."

Younger nodded. "I was tendin' bar there about that time. Idaho City was a rip-snorter in them days. Wasn't Lew Rogan mixed up with some bogus-dust passers? I mean the ones that got lynched at Wahoe Ferry. The Pickett Corral gang, we called 'em."

Abe Earnshaw's lips drooped in a grim grin. "You've got it kinda mixed up, Jess. Rogan didn't have anything to do with that Pickett Corral gang. Chuck and Alex Stewart headed up that crowd." Earnshaw narrowed his eyes wisely. "I oughta know, seein' as I was one of the twenty vigilantes that strung 'em up."

Marcus Lindsay, although he made no comment, well remembered that raid at Wahoe Ferry—a sensation which had high-lighted the raw and lusty life of early Idaho.

"Bogus dust?" Paul Stanley asked confusedly.

70

"Gold dust was legal tender in them days," Earnshaw explained, "in all the Idaho diggings. Every counter and bar had scales to weigh it. You bought your grub and powder and whisky with it. Most Idaho miners never carried any money at all. But they all had a pouch of dust and the price per ounce was posted in every store and bank.

"Then a gang of sharks began bringin' in bogus. You could hardly tell it from the real stuff. Most of it was manufactured in San Francisco by cutting bars of lead into tiny specks and galvanizin' 'em with gold. Fooled purty nigh everybody, sometimes even when they used the nitric acid test."

"How did they pass it?" Warren asked. It was a cloudy night and the only light came from the fire. An owl hooted from the creek bank cottonwoods.

"Just like you'd pass counterfeit money—by payin' bills with it," Earnshaw said.

"Lots of it was worked off by the deposit trick," Jess Younger remembered. "Nearly every roadside storekeeper in Idaho kept a can or jar with deposits of gold dust in it. Just like a bank. A bogus passer would come by and have the storeman weigh his dust. The storeman would give him a receipt and then dump his dust in a jar with a lot of other deposits. Later the guy would come back to claim his deposit. The storekeeper would weigh it out to him in real gold."

"During the Sixties," Earnshaw went on, "it was the biggest gyp game in Idaho. It had hoss stealing and stage robbing beat all hollow. The Pickett Corral gang did most of it and they hung out in a stout log cabin near Wahoe Ferry right about where the Payette River joins the Snake. They got so bold and sassy there was only one thing left to do, and we done it. We organized a committee of vigilantes and whanged down on 'em."

"Hung 'em all, didn't you?" Younger prompted.

The bullwhacker tamped tobacco in his pipe. "Nope. If you'll think back you'll recollect we only hung the leaders, Chuck and Alex Stewart. Shot all the rest of 'em except one, and we gave *him* twenty-four hours to get out of Idaho. He did, and he ain't been seen since."

"Why," Paul Stanley asked, "did you give him a better shake than the others?"

"Because the man we wanted most of all wasn't there at all. I mean the one who supplied them with the bogus dust and kept it coming from Frisco. We were pretty sure he operated out of Idaho City but we didn't know who he was. All the Pickett Corral gang did was pass the stuff for him and take their cut of the profit. So we told the last man we'd let him have twenty-four hours to get out of the territory provided he'd name the real head of the ring."

"And did he?"

"He said he didn't know the man's name. But he told us when and where we could find him. There was a log cabin with an iron roof on More's Creek at the mouth of Buzzard Gulch where the man met the Stewarts once a month to dole out some more bogus. The next appointment to meet him was just three days away. If we nabbed the man when he showed up there we'd find plenty of bogus on him."

"So you laid for the guy at the More's Creek cabin?"

"Yep. Five of us hid in the brush there from dawn till midnight. It was right on the stage road that runs from Idaho City to Boise. We saw lots of people and wagons go by that day. But nobody went into the cabin. Only one man stopped. He was horseback and we all knew him well. He had a first-rate reputation in those diggings. When he came opposite the cabin he stopped his horse but didn't dismount. Just sat his saddle half a minute, quiet like. Then he rode on toward Boise City and we didn't think nothin' more about him. Just kept hidin' there waitin' for the right man to come along."

"You finally nabbed him?"

"Nope. We stayed there till past midnight and nobody went into the cabin. So we broke up and went home. Coupla weeks later a few of us at an Idaho City bar got to talkin' about the man who'd stopped his horse near the cabin without goin' in. Maybe he'd intended to go in but at the last minute got a hunch he was being watched. Maybe one of us wasn't hid good enough. In that case he'd ride right on.

"He had a house in Idaho City and if he was our man he'd be likely to have some bogus stowed away there. We had no authority to search it ourselves. Fact is we had to walk soft on account of that lynch party at Wahoe Ferry. The governor was raisin' hell about it. So we decided to make the search legal. The only lawman in town that day was a constable named Rogan. So we gave Rogan a few drinks and talked him into searchin' the man's house for bogus dust."

Jess Younger whacked a fist into palm. "I remember now. I knew Lew Rogan fit in somewhere. He searched the man's house and didn't find a thing."

"He *said* he didn't," Earnshaw agreed cryptically.

There was an implication in his tone which Marcus Lindsay didn't miss. He asked curiously: "You mean maybe he found some bogus but didn't report it?"

"We didn't begin wonderin' about that till a year later," Earnshaw confided. "It was a year later when Rogan got fired on suspicion of taking a bribe to let a prisoner escape. If he took hush money once, maybe he took it that other time— from Wade Canby!"

Canby! The name startled Lindsay. Yes, in those days Canby's engineering office was at Idaho City. Could he have been supply agent for the Pickett Corral gang?

This same Canby was about to marry Lois Lindsay!

Could he, Marcus Lindsay, let it happen? If Canby was the right sort, yes. If he wasn't, no. He couldn't let Lois blight her life, and the boy's, by marriage to a man with an outlaw past. Marcus Lindsay wanted nothing for himself. For Lois he wanted everything—at least contentment and an untroubled future.

Far from untroubled himself, Lindsay left the fire and spread his blankets on the creek bank. For most of the night he lay staring up at the darkness, thinking about Constable Rogan and the unsolved mystery of long ago. Had a respected engineer of Idaho City really pulled strings for the Wahoe Ferry gang? Had Rogan really found a supply of bogus in his house when he'd searched there? Had Rogan accepted a bribe to keep quiet about it?

There was no proof—nor any thin ground for suspicion except that Wade Canby *had* stopped his horse in front of a certain cabin on a certain day, and that Rogan *had* later turned out to be a bribe-taker.

For restless hours Marcus Lindsay thought about it, and before morning he came to a decision. He'd go on to Boise City but for a different reason than the one which had pulled at him until now. He must go there to ferret out the truth about Wade Canby, and if the truth was ugly to somehow warn Lois before it was too late.

Not an easy thing to do. For a nameless, faceless wagonhand an almost impossible mission! Yet the challenge of it gave Marcus Lindsay a new vigor—and for the first time in ten years an exciting purpose in life.

CHAPTER VII

Each afternoon at three o'clock a stagecoach from Kelton was due in Boise City and in good weather was likely to be on time. For the first several days after her arrival Nan Stanley never failed to be there when the coach pulled up in front of the Overland Hotel. Always a crowd was on hand, some to meet incoming passengers.

Nan's question was always the same—when and where had the stage passed her brothers and their cattle drive? It was no use asking the driver who had only come the last fifty miles. But there was always a passenger or two who'd come all the way from Kelton.

"We passed lots of landseekers headin' this way, Miss, but no trail herd. Might be your menfolks are keepin' a mile or so off the road to get better grass."

It was the same report for six days but on the seventh there was news. "Yep, Miss, we caught up with a small cow drive about fifteen mile the other side of Albion. Looked like about three hun'erd head of young she-stuff. Outfit had two drovers and a wagon man."

A stagecoach two days later brought a letter postmarked at the Albion relay station:

Dear Sis:

We're about seventy-five miles out of Kelton and right on time. Heard about that brush you had with road agents. Tell that cowboy who outgunned them we owe him a heap of thanks and we'll sure look him up when we get there. Sorry to hear those crooks ganged up on him later in town. The stock's in good flesh and that wagoneer we hired at Kelton is a peach. He's got an ugly face but a heart of gold—and he can cook darn near as good as he can skin mules. We offered him a permanent job. Take care of yourself and look for us in about two weeks.

Love,
Paul.

Nan was reading it in the Overland lobby when Lois Lindsay came in with her nine-year-old boy. The boy had rosy cheeks and blue eyes. His mother's eyes were brown. Nan had met the boy several days ago when Lois had stopped in to inquire about Verne Hallam.

"How's he getting along?" Lois asked now.

"He still takes his meals in bed," Nan reported. "But the doctor says he can come down to the dining room tomorrow." She added brightly: "I've a message for him from my brothers. Listen."

Nan read aloud the note from Paul.

"Then what are we waiting for?" Lois Lindsay exclaimed. "Since we've a message for him, let's deliver it at once."

They went upstairs and down a corridor to room 237. A knock brought a prompt "Come in" from Verne Hallam. But to Nan's surprise the door was opened by a visitor already there.

"John Hailey!" Lois greeted him as an old and intimate friend. "What are *you* doing here? Nan, I want you to meet a man who's sure to be governor of Idaho some day. Right now he operates stage lines all over Utah, Idaho and Oregon. John, you ought to be ashamed of yourself for letting this poor girl get held up. She'd already suffered enough, riding from Kelton on one of your rattle-trap coaches."

Hailey, a solid, bronzed man with kindly gray eyes, shook hands with Nan and smiled as he answered Lois Lindsay. "What most mortifies me, Lois, is to learn that this young man here," he nodded toward Verne who was sitting upright in bed, "had received no more than a perfunctory thanks from my local agent. So I came to make partial amends."

"Look what he gave me!" Verne held up a new and shiny leather wallet. "It's got exactly what those bums took off me. Ninety-four bucks."

Nan knew that the thugs who'd beaten Verne to within an inch of his life had also made off with his wallet.

"Not only that," the cowboy went on happily, "but the stage line's payin' my hotel and doctor bill." A week in bed had restored his rubicund color and except for a bandaged head there was no visible evidence of his misadventure.

"It's the least we can do," John Hailey said, "for a man who rescued one of our coaches and two very lovely passengers. By the way, Lois, when's the big event coming off?"

"The tenth of July," Lois told him. It was now past the middle of June.

"House wedding or church?"

"I'll be married at home, John Hailey. And you'll be among the invited."

"Good. A lucky guy, that Wade Canby."

The name brought a memory to Verne Hallam and the grin left his face. It was a memory of Lew Rogan slyly slipping a note into Canby's pocket. Somehow the incident seemed to put Canby at a level less than worthy to become the husband of a woman like Mrs. Lindsay.

When Verne looked again at John Hailey the stage line operator had a hand on the head of Mark Lindsay and was tousling the boy's hair affectionately. "How would you like to drive one of my stages when you grow up, young man?"

"No sir." The boy's answer was respectful but firm. "I don't want to be a stage driver. I want to be a cowboy like Verne Hallam."

His mother laughed. "Then maybe you can get

a job with Nan's brothers. By the time you grow up they could have one of the biggest ranches in Idaho. Show Verne the letter, Nan."

While John Hailey and Lois Lindsay chatted near the doorway, Nan stood by the bed and read Paul's letter to Verne. This was the third time she'd been in to see him—once with Mrs. Lindsay, and once with Jim Agnew at Doctor Eph Smith's house during the three days Verne had been hospitalized there. Agnew, no less grateful than John Hailey, was boarding Verne's horse and pack mare free of charge at his livery barn.

"What about the road agents?" Verne asked. "Did the posse ever get wind of 'em?"

Nan shook her head. "Some think they're hiding up on Shaw's Mountain. Others think they rode southeast toward Utah. A sheepherder saw four riders by starlight crossing the Snake River near Glenn's Ferry."

The four, Verne thought, could be the three stage robbers reinforced by the chunky, middle-aged man who'd decoyed Verne to the Grove Street house. That man would hardly dare stay here in town, since the victim could identify him to the law. As for the two bruisers who'd jumped him in the hallway, Verne was less sure. There'd only been brief glimpses of their faces in dim lamplight. "Maybe I'd know them and maybe I wouldn't," Verne had told Marshal Orlando Robbins.

"Keep away from that rifle, Mark!" The admonition came from the boy's mother as she saw him about to pick up Verne's repeating Winchester.

The light of hero worship was on the boy's face as he looked at Verne. "How many Indians have you killed with it?" he asked.

"None," Verne told him. "Most of the Indians I ever ran into were nice people. A heap nicer than some white folks I know."

"I can say the same myself," John Hailey added.

Lois said gently: "There are good Indians and bad Indians, Mark. White people are the same way, good and bad. Most of our troubles in Idaho come from bad white men."

"That's not what Mr. Canby says, Mother. He says the only good Indians are dead Indians."

Verne saw shock on Lois Lindsay's usually calm face. "I'm sure Wade didn't really mean that, Mark. He's kind and fair. Nan, I think we'd better be running along now." She turned to Verne. "If you're well enough to take a carriage ride by day after tomorrow, we'll come by again and show you the town."

When his visitors were gone Verne was left alone thinking pleasantly of Nan, and of the Lindsays and John Hailey, but not at all pleasantly of a man named Wade Canby.

If Canby was kind and fair, why would he give

a nine-year-old boy the idea that Indians were things to be shot at and killed like wild animals? And if he wasn't, why would a high-minded lady want to marry him?

Two afternoons later the high-minded lady's coachman drove her open carriage up Main Street with Verne Hallam between Lois and Nan on the rear seat. The boy Mark sat up front with the driver. From Sixth to Eighth both sides of Main were lined with immigrant wagons, resupplying themselves from the stores after a hard trek westward along the Overland road.

"When my people came out in 1866," Lois remembered, "we had to follow the old Oregon Trail across Wyoming and over South Pass. There was no railroad then. Now it's much easier. People can ship their wagons and household goods by rail to Kelton, Utah. From there they can follow the Salisbury-Hailey stage road here to the Boise basin, or on to Oregon—the way your brothers are coming, Nan."

"All these wagon people will take out homesteads, I suppose," Verne suggested.

"Probably. They're landseekers. The goldseekers have stopped coming. Most of these immigrants will file original homesteads—a few will refile on relinquishments from discouraged homesteaders who aren't rugged and stubborn enough to prove up."

They passed the Stone Jug at Sixth and Main. "Wade Canby has an office upstairs," Lois said to Verne. "You must go up and see him some time. Good afternoon, Governor." Governor Biggerstaff, chatting on the walk with the commandant at Fort Boise, waved his hat as the carriage passed on.

It turned finally into Idaho Street, passing the Bonanza gambling house, then rolling on east past a dozen disreputable saloons and a pair of noisy burlesque theaters. Painted women peering from upper windows made Lois correct the coachman's choice of route. "Get off this street, Horace. Better look straight ahead, Nan, or you'll be shocked. China Alley runs back of this row of saloons," she told Verne.

At Fifth Street the coachman turned north and at the mouth of China Alley passed a shabby saloon labeled SMEED'S PLACE.

A man with a stubble of red beard on his moon-shaped face was lounging at the door of it and to Verne he seemed vaguely familiar. He was sure he'd seen the man before but the carriage had gone a block farther before he remembered where.

Even then he couldn't be certain. The doorway loafer had looked a good deal like one of the toughs who'd jumped him in the Grove Street house. Verne's first impulse was to ask the coachman to turn back and give him a second look.

But it might alarm the ladies and he decided not to. Besides, Verne wasn't armed and he was in no physical shape to confront his assailants alone at a dive like Smeed's. As soon as he could part company with the ladies he'd report his suspicion to Marshal Robbins.

"Drive out to Fort Boise, Horace," Mrs. Lindsay directed. "Then circle back past the territorial penitentiary."

Shadows were long by the time they'd driven by both the military post and the prison. Then the hostess took her guests along the capital's shaded show street, Warm Springs Avenue. Lawns there had spiked iron fences, fountains and sweeping carriage drives.

Finally they turned into Lois Lindsay's own driveway and stopped at her door. "I told Helga to have supper ready for us," she said.

It was late dusk when she sent her guests home in the carriage. By then Verne had all but forgotten the face he'd seen in a saloon doorway. Dinner at a house more elegant than any he'd ever entered before, in the company of two charming ladies and a boy who looked upon him as a hero, had made it an experience almost unreal to a cowboy who'd been spreading his bedroll on creek banks for forty-odd nights on his way from Kansas to western Idaho.

"How lucky we are to know her!" Nan murmured. "She's so kind and generous and beautiful. And yet . . ."

"And yet what?"

"Sometimes I sense a sadness back of all her gaiety and charm. As though she was forcing it in order to forget something unpleasant. I asked Mr. Agnew about it and he thinks she's never gotten over a horrible tragedy which took her husband's life, a long time ago. Maybe it's why she's gone all these ten years without remarrying."

"But now," Verne said, "she *is* remarrying. A fella named Canby. You've met him, Nan. How do you size him up?"

"He's awfully good looking," the girl said. "And he has charming manners."

Verne looked sideways at her. "Is that all?"

"I don't think he's nearly good enough for her, if that's what you mean."

"That's what I mean," Verne said bluntly. A somber preoccupation possessed him until the coachman let them out at the Overland Hotel.

After saying goodnight to Nan at the foot of the lobby stairs Verne hurried up Main to a street-level office whose door bore the names:

E. S. CHASE,
UNITED STATES MARSHAL
ORLANDO ROBBINS,
DEPUTY U. S. MARSHAL

Chase wasn't in. But Robbins was, and he listened gravely to Verne's report of the red-stubbled face he'd seen in the saloon doorway at the corner of Fifth and China Alley.

"It's a tough joint, Smeed's," Robbins said. "The night barkeep's Dutch Henry, who once served a term for passing bogus." The marshal used the cuff of his coat to buff a brass badge, then stood up to buckle on a gunbelt.

"Want me to get mine?" Verne offered. "I've got a forty-five holster gun and a 44-40 saddle gun in my room."

"Leave 'em there," Robbins cut in. "You're in no shape for a gun pull. Besides, I can handle anything in this town. You just come along and point out the man if he's still there."

They left the office and walked down Eighth to Idaho, turning east there. Looking at Orlando Robbins's calm, mild face it was hard for Verne to believe what he'd heard about the man—that he'd successively held the offices of town marshal, deputy sheriff, sheriff, warden of the penitentiary and deputy United States marshal, and that he had a reputation for dogged persistence when trailing outlaws and a record of success which had made him famous all over the West.

Three blocks down the noisy, red-lighted street brought them to Fifth, where they turned half a block north to the mouth of a narrow, smelly alley with Chinese shops and dives fronting it.

"Enough opium smoked in 'em," Robbins said, "to drug an army. Here we are, Hallam. If your man's at the bar, point a finger and leave the rest to me."

Verne had never seen anyone more confident and fearless than Orlando Robbins as the marshal walked into Smeed's place. Verne kept at his heels, his eyes sweeping a pine board bar. Most of the bar customers were shabby third-raters. No women were in sight. A cheap joint like this would make poor hunting for the kind of women who lived near Fifth and Idaho. The floor was sawdust and the spittoons were tin.

The fat, balding bartender at once became obsequious when he saw Robbins. "Evenin', Colonel. Anything I can do for yuh?"

"Nothing, Dutch," Robbins said shortly. "Just a routine check to see if you've got any trouble-makers here."

His voice made every face at the bar turn toward them and Verne, by the light of two kerosene lamps which hung from the saloon's rafters, saw that none of them was the face he was looking for. This afternoon's red-stubbled loafer wasn't here now. Neither was the decoy man who'd called himself Baker.

A slight shake of Verne's head conveyed those facts to Robbins.

The officer was clearly disappointed. "Half of these bums have been in my jail at one time or another," he said covertly to Verne. "But there's nothing I can pick 'em up for now."

As he advanced to the bar the men lining it made way for him. Three of them scurried out through the street door and a fourth made a slinking exit through a side door at the rear, which gave into China Alley. Most of them huddled either at the head or at the foot of the bar.

Robbins spoke blandly to the bartender. "Heard from your brother-in-law lately?"

Dutch Henry averted his eyes and mumbled, "I ain't got no brother-in-law."

"That's funny. According to the records you've got a sister named Belle. She married Floyd Plover, didn't she?"

"If she did it's none of my business. Belle goes her way and I go mine."

"What about a guy with a red-stubbled chin? Face like a full moon. Has he been in here lately?"

"Not that I noticed. Lots of red-heads come in here and most of 'em need a shave."

"Which of your regular customers calls himself Bob Baker?"

"Never heard of him."

A pitch of alarm was in the bartender's denial and Verne saw his eyes fix on the side door at the rear. A man was entering there from China Alley. His round face had a three-day reddish beard and Verne saw that he was the man who'd lounged in the street doorway this afternoon as the Lindsay carriage passed. Verne was sure that he was one of the pair who'd slugged him in the lamp-lighted hallway.

"There he is, Marshal!" Verne pointed toward the alley entrance.

As Orlando Robbins turned that way, two fast pistol shots boomed from somewhere near the head of the bar. Any one of a dozen customers huddled there could have fired them. Two kerosene lamps crashed to the sawdust floor and the room was instantly dark.

In the darkness Verne heard feet scampering toward the two exits. He moved toward the alley door himself, groping blindly, bumping into one stampeding customer and stumbling over the leg of another. A boot kicked his shin and an elbow poked into his ribs. It was a pandemonium of escape and over it Orlando Robbins's voice came quietly from the dark. "Block the street door if you can, Hallam. Everybody else stay put. You too, Dutch."

By the sound he made the marshal was moving to block the alley exit. Verne turned the other way, groping, but he knew it was too late. The noise of scampering boots had stopped. Again Marshal Robbins spoke quietly. "Make a light for us, Dutch. A lamp, a candle, anything. And be quick about it."

As Verne reached the vicinity of the street door

his outstretched hand punched someone in the face. Immediately the man grappled with him and as Verne wriggled to get free a gun barrel cracked him on the head. It didn't hurt much because the quarters were too close to give the man a free swing.

Then a light flared as Dutch Henry held a match to a candle on the backbar. Three candles in a row were lighted one by one and Verne saw with chagrin who he was grappling with.

"Let him go, Uncle Billy. It's the cowboy Hallam." This from Robbins at the rear.

Verne drew back and saw Night Constable Billy Paxton standing in front of him with a drawn gun. "Makes twice I've walked in on you, boy," the constable said with a grin. "Seems like you're always in a ruckus of some kind. I heard a couple of shots in here."

"Someone gunned out the lights," Robbins explained dourly, "and everybody skeedaddled."

In the candlelight Verne saw the barroom was empty except for Dutch Henry behind the bar, and Paxton, Robbins and himself in front of it. "I got a glimpse of that red-stubbled face," Robbins said. "Never saw it before. Put a name to it, Dutch, or I'll run you in."

Dutch Henry gave them an innocent stare. "You mean that bum who was comin' in from the alley when the lights went out? I don't know him, Colonel. Honest to Gawd I don't."

"Who was it gunned out the lights?" Robbins demanded.

The man spread fat, moist hands and shrugged. "I was lookin' the other way, Colonel. Didn't see who done that shootin'. If I knew I'd tell you. And that's the truth, so help me!"

Robbins and Paxton exchanged hopeless looks. It was a stalemate and they knew it.

After a minute of dull quiet the alley door opened. This time a sallow Chinese with his shirttail reaching to the knees of his baggy pants came in with a gallon pail in hand. The candlelight fell eerily on him as he set the pail on the bar. "One can beer, please. Not all suds like last time, please."

Smeed's was doing business again.

CHAPTER VIII

Day after day the outfit of Paul and Stanley Warren made dust along the trail from Kelton. In the neighborhood of the Albion station it veered west across bushless barrens, keeping from five to fifteen miles south of, and roughly parallel to, the Snake River. Sometimes from his wagon seat Marcus Lindsay caught a distant glimpse of the great winding river but usually it was hidden by its own deep-cut badlands. Always he kept well ahead of the cattle herd.

On the eighth night out of Kelton the wagoneer picked a camp site near the Rock Creek relay station. By the time the herd came up he had supper sizzling.

"We're out of shortening," he said. "I'd better walk up to the store and get some."

Rock Creek was a swing station where the Kelton-to-Boise City stages changed drivers and where meals were served to passengers. In addition to a corral and dining room it had a trading store, post office and bar. As Lindsay arrived there a Kelton-bound stage came up, trace chains jingling. The hostler had four fresh horses ready and harnessed. Six passengers and

93

a driver swarmed into the station for supper.

A bundle of Boise City newspapers was tossed off and Lindsay bought one. After picking up a can of lard he stood by the station stove to listen in on talk.

"Did they ever ketch up with those Indian Creek stage robbers?" the stationmaster asked the incoming driver.

"Nope. The posse turned back empty-handed. What you got for supper?"

"Mutton and beans. Anything new at the Capital?"

"Bunch of convicts busted out of the pen and ain't been caught yet. Might've headed this way. Bill Stewart's contestin' for the governorship, claimin' Biggerstaff wasn't elected legally. Coupla gunfights on Idaho Street and a slit throat in China Alley. Somebody shot the lights out in Smeed's place to keep a guy from gettin' pinched. Pete Keeney shot Dave Adamson through the belly on account of they both claimed the same calf. Lots of landseeker wagons goin' through, mostly headin' for Oregon."

Marcus Lindsay lingered a while longer, hoping to hear mention of Wade Canby. Checking on Canby was his main goal now. Was what he'd heard from Earnshaw at the Raft Creek camp mere idle gossip?

The Boise City *Statesman* he'd bought had Canby's card ad in it:

WADE CANBY
CONSULTING ENGINEER & MINERALOGIST
OFFICE IN CURTIS BLOCK
MAIN STREET, BOISE CITY

Lindsay walked back to camp and after supper gave the paper a thorough reading by lantern light. In a column of local briefs he found two items of interest.

Lois Lindsay of Warm Springs Avenue brought her son Mark back from the Hubbard farm down the valley, where the boy visited while Mrs. Lindsay went to Rocky Bar on a business trip.

* * *

Verne Hallam, the Kansas cowboy who tangled with stage robbers on the Overland Trail, has been given a special permit to carry a gun for personal protection. Judging by what happened at a certain Grove Street house, he'll need it. He and Miss Nan Stanley, who arrived on the stage with him, were the guests of John Hailey for dinner last night.

Lindsay pointed out the latter item to Warren Stanley, who whistled and called to his brother. "Looks like Sis is making friends fast, Paul."

Paul was more interested in a page of advertisements. In a listing of farms and ranches for sale he found the following:

> Fenced section eight miles below town on south side of Boise River, improved with six-room house, sheds, corrals and small meadow of native hay. Good cottonwood shade. For sale or lease on reasonable terms. See John Huntoon, Cashier, First National Bank of Idaho, Boise City.

"Sounds good, Warren. Maybe we could lease with an option to buy." The prospect absorbed them all evening.

The next day they made fourteen miles and the day after that they made twelve. Lindsay, keeping his wagon well ahead, sighted a deer on the second evening out of Rock Creek. He was skinning it when the brothers drew up at the night's campsite.

"Beats jackrabbit," Paul agreed as he chewed venison steak. Since leaving Raft Creek their only fresh meat had been rabbit.

"When and where do we cross the Snake?"

"At a place called Glenn's Ferry," Paul said, "accordin' to that freighter we passed today. He said we oughta hit Salmon Falls by noon tomorrow and from there it's only about thirty miles to the ferry."

When Lindsay drew up at the Salmon Falls station a noon later a Kelton-bound coach was changing horses. Among the passengers who got out to stretch legs was a man Lindsay had known twelve years ago in Boise City—Judge Milton Kelly, then a prominent attorney and politician, and now publisher of the Boise City *Statesman*. Lindsay was buying the *Statesman*'s latest issue at the Salmon Falls counter when Kelly spoke heartily at his elbow. "Never mind paying for it, stranger. It's on me." He tossed a small coin on the counter. "Is that your herd of cattle I see coming up the trail?"

The wagoneer's momentary alarm subsided when he saw that he wasn't recognized. "No. I'm just the mule skinner. Coupla lads named Stanley own those cows."

Kelly's eyes narrowed. "The Stanley boys, huh? They've got a kid sister who went on ahead by stage, haven't they?"

"That's right. Thanks for the paper."

"Read my editorial on the Biggerstaff-Stewart feud." Again Kelly's eyes narrowed. "Haven't I seen you before somewhere?"

"Reckon not. My name's Gresham and I'm new to Idaho."

"Well, tell those Stanley boys they made a good pick comin' to the Boise basin. It'll be a real cattle country some day and the sooner we start stockin' it the better. Stockin' it not only

97

with cattle but with people. People like those immigrant folks over there." Kelly pointed across the road to three westbound covered wagons. The three families were stopping here a few days to rest their horses, mend their wagons and wash clothes with the first soft water they'd encountered in a hundred miles.

"On their way to Oregon," Lindsay suggested.

"Maybe. Or maybe they'll settle in Idaho like the Stanleys. What counts is that they're landseekers. First came the goldseekers and now come the landseekers—and the land'll last longer than the gold. The gold towns like Idaho City'll be ghost towns, but the land towns like Boise City'll be solid, growing family towns."

Kelly was turning away when an afterthought made him swing back with a word of advice. "Tell the Stanley boys if they've got any cash on 'em, they'll be smart to ship it ahead of them by Wells Fargo express to the Boise City bank. Lots of bad actors along this Overland Trail. Never a week passes but some stage or wagon outfit gets stuck up."

"I'll tell them," Lindsay promised.

He watered his mules at the Salmon Falls trough and waited for the drive to catch up. When it did he relayed Milton Kelly's advice to Paul Stanley.

"Sounds like a good idea to me. What do you say, Warren?"

"We've only got a couple of hundred in cash, Paul."

"But no use taking a chance with it," Paul said. "And while we're at it we might as well send along that bank draft in the same package."

"Why?" Warren demurred. "Nobody could cash it but us."

"Just the same," Paul argued, "I'd a heap rather have that money waitin' for us when we get there. If we lose the check we might have to wait a month before the Salt Lake City bank makes it good."

With a shrug his brother conceded the point. The bank draft was included with the cash in a neat, tight Wells Fargo express package to be shipped out on the next Boise City–bound stage. The Salmon Falls stationmaster gave a receipt for it and Mark Lindsay mounted his wagon to drive on.

"You'll find good camp water and shade," a hostler told him, "just this side of Pilgrim's Hill."

A morning later the Stanley drive crossed Pilgrim's Hill and veered northeasterly toward Glenn's Ferry. A road sign told them that they were now in Owyhee County and again, from high points with a good view to the north, Lindsay was able to catch glimpses of the mighty Snake River. It was at full June tide now and he was glad he'd be crossing on a ferry. The Stanley boys would have to swim their mounts across behind a swimming herd of cattle.

By sundown he was on level ground again and at twilight he found camp water and shade. The creek was small but its cottonwood cover was generous. Lindsay picketed the remounts and turned his mules loose, knowing they wouldn't stray far from the horses. The herd arrived presently and by dark had bedded down along the creeklet.

"Have you thought about that offer we made, John?" Paul asked over supper coffee. "I mean about working for us permanently?"

"I'll take it." Lindsay said it with decision. Living on a ranch near Boise City would give him a chance to check on Wade Canby—and since confronting Milton Kelly he had less fear of being recognized there.

"Fine and dandy!" Paul exclaimed. "First thing we'll do'll be to run down that ad about an improved section eight miles below town. Sounds like Home Sweet Home to me. Won't be long now. Boise City's less than a hundred miles beyond Glenn's Ferry."

And the ferry, Lindsay knew as he made his bed that night, was only nine miles beyond this camp. A rider from the Bliss Ranch, across the Snake River, had passed his wagon this afternoon and told him that. That and something else.

"We had four horses lifted out of our corral the other night. The four played-out broncs they left behind make us think they could be the Floyd Plover gang. Three of 'em jibe with descriptions of horses ridden by road agents at Indian Creek two weeks ago. Maybe you read about it in the papers."

"I heard talk about it," Lindsay said.

"So those jiggers could be close by somewhere. If you've got anything worth stealing, better keep a close watch."

Worth stealing from the Stanley outfit were three hundred cows, four good horses, two mules, two rifles, one holster gun, two saddles, a wagonload of goods and one shotgun. As a precaution Marcus Lindsay took the shotgun to bed with him and chose a spot about fifty yards down the grove from the wagon.

For a while he lay listening to the night sounds, the stirring of restless cattle, the champing of picketed horses, the hoot of an owl, low talk from the Stanley brothers up by the wagon. Then the fire went out and they too went to bed.

A gunshot wakened Lindsay. He sat up in his blankets and reached for the shotgun. The rasping voice was one he'd never heard before. "Don't try any monkey business, Mister, or you'll get the same medicine. Round up their guns, boys."

Other strange voices reached Lindsay and he knew that invaders had held up the camp. Then came the subdued voice of Warren Stanley. "Are you hurt bad, Paul?"

"I only nicked him," the rasping voice said. "Next time he'll get it good and you too. Where do you keep the mazuma? The five thousand dollars?"

"In a bank," Warren's voice said.

"That ain't what we heard. Search him, boys. And one of you better round up the wagoneer. Light a lantern and look around for him."

Lindsay, fully dressed except for his hat and boots, took the shotgun and crawled stealthily away from his blankets. Both the shotgun barrels were loaded with duckshot but he had no extra shells. There were four thieves, according to the Bliss Ranch rider. Even if he downed two of them there'd still be two left.

Just how he could deal with them Marcus Lindsay didn't know. For the moment his job was to keep under cover. He could see a lighted lantern winding in and out among the cottonwoods as one of the robbers searched for his bed.

"Here it is, Floyd," the searcher shouted. "But it's empty."

"Stop using names, you lunkhead!"

A third voice reported: "Nothing but chicken feed in their wallets."

"Then they've got the dough stashed in the wagon. Frisk it good."

Warren Stanley spoke again. "You're wasting your time. We keep our money in a bank."

"Yeah? Either you're a liar or Lew is. Take that wagon apart, boys. Shake out the duffel bags. And pick up that wagon skinner. He's bound to be around somewhere."

In the darkness Lindsay crawled to the creek and slid down into the bed of it. His bootless feet squinched in mud there. Then the man with the lantern came to the creek and leaned over for a look into it. Lindsay flattended himself against an overhanging bank, holding his breath.

When the man was gone he groped his way cautiously along the bank to get opposite the wagon.

Clearly this was the Floyd Plover gang who'd held up an Overland stage two weeks ago. Apparently a fourth outlaw had joined the original three. They'd mentioned someone named Lew. Lew seemed to be a tipster who'd led them to believe that the Stanleys carried five thousand in cash. According to the *Statesman*, there'd been a man named Lew on the stage with Nan Stanley. A Lew Rogan.

"Keep looking," the head robber snapped impatiently. "Take that duffel apart piece by piece. The dough's bound to be there." The man's tone took a snarling pitch as the minutes went by with no cash loot uncovered.

"They've got four good horses and two good

saddles," a man reported. "Looks like that and their guns is about all we can ride away with."

Lindsay crept up the sloping bank and lay flat on the grass, his shotgun aimed over the bank's rim. A short, stocky man stood not a dozen yards away and it would be easy to riddle him with duckshot. With his second barrel Lindsay could down the tall, thin man who held a gun on Warren Stanley. But it would leave the shotgun empty and the two surviving outlaws would shoot down both Lindsay and the Stanleys.

The man at the wagon lighted a second lantern to help his search there. He was pitching out bags, bedding, boxes and crates, any of which might hold hidden money. A fourth man was off in the grove with a lantern, searching for the wagon driver.

Paul, helpless from a gunshot wound, lay near the crumpled blankets from which he'd sprung, perhaps suddenly alarmed by the sound of a stealthy intrusion. He might have snatched a gun from under his pillow and been shot before he could use it—that would be the shot which had wakened Lindsay. It would also have aroused Warren, but too late. Warren stood disarmed about five baffling paces from a tree against which his rifle leaned.

The man at the wagon was dumping out the contents of bags and boxes, scattering them on the ground. "Maybe it ain't here," he muttered presently. "Maybe it was a bum steer we got about that five thousand dollars."

After a few minutes more of the fruitless search he looked balefully at the Stanleys. "What we gonna do with 'em?" he muttered.

"They heard you use my name, didn't they?" the stocky man reminded him. "They can describe us, can't they? Doesn't leave us any choice, does it?"

"Reckon you're right," the man at the wagon agreed. "It don't leave us no choice. We should've wore masks and kept our mouths shut." He cocked a gun and advanced to stand by the outlaw who covered Warren Stanley. "We might as well leave 'em have it right now and be done."

CHAPTER IX

"Not yet, you dopes!" the heavyset leader snapped. The lantern light let Lindsay make out a scar which slanted down his forehead. "It won't do any good unless we get all three of 'em. One mouth can blab as easy as three. Ferd, put that fella to sleep so you can go help hunt for the driver."

The man called Ferd hit hard with the barrel of his gun and dropped Warren in a lump to the ground. Warren lay motionless and stunned. Beyond him Lindsay could see the dim shapes of four saddled horses standing cock-kneed with reins hanging, and on which the outlaws had ridden up. No doubt they were the horses stolen from the Bliss Ranch corral across the Snake River.

"Now look, Ferd," Floyd Plover reasoned shrewdly. "The only chance that wagon skinner'd have to get away'd be to sneak up to where they picketed their horses. We spotted 'em as we rode up, remember? They're about a hundred yards down crik."

"Yeh," Ferd said, "they unsaddled 'em right there. Worth maybe five hundred dollars, them saddles and horses."

"We'll take 'em along for remounts," Plover

said. "But first we got to knock over that wagoneer. Go to the pickets and lay low there, Ferd. When he slips up to get himself a horse, gun him down. Then we can do the same to these other guys and ride out of here."

Ferd disappeared down creek through the trees. "Now let's you and me look through this wagon gear," Plover said to the man with the lantern.

As they ransacked through bags and boxes, the two men were so close together that Lindsay wondered if he could get both with one shot. The shotgun had a scatter bore and a choke bore. By using the first on two men, he'd still have a shell left for the other two.

Then a saner plan occurred to Marcus Lindsay. One man had a lantern and was scouting the grove for him. The other was in ambush at the pickets to waylay him if he tried to escape by saddle.

Lindsay, who'd selected this campsite in daylight, could find his way around it better than anyone else. He knew that a side gully came into the creek just below the picketed mounts. Still in his bootless feet he slipped cautiously down the muddy creek bed, shotgun ready in case he came suddenly upon the scouting lanternman.

He heard the scout and saw the gleam of his lantern. Keeping out of sight himself Lindsay moved to the mouth of the small gully and slipped up it. Its bed was dry.

The whirr of a rattlesnake gave him pause. Holding his breath he detoured around the sound and got safely above it. The next sound reaching him was the champing of a tied horse. As he peered over the gully's rim the starlight showed him four equine shapes. Beyond he saw a big, white-boled cottonwood with the form of a man crouched at the foot of it. The man would be Ferd and there'd be a gun in his hand. Four stock saddles, each with a blanket and bridle, lay nearby.

Ferd was there to kill on sight. *By rights I ought to treat him the same way.*

But Lindsay didn't. Instead he moved another forty yards up the gully. Then he crawled out of it and advanced into the grove, circling to get beyond the big cottonwood tree where Ferd waited.

Lindsay came up as soundlessly as a moccasined Indian behind it until only the tree trunk itself separated him from Ferd. He could hear the man breathing.

Marcus Lindsay had never been a man of violence. In all the ten years of his masquerade as John Gresham he'd never fired a weapon at anything but wild game. For the first of those lonely years fear of being recognized and exposed as the husband of Lois Lindsay had kept him peculiarly shy and meek.

Now here he was with a shotgun in his hands

in a life or death showdown with four outlaws—killers who'd already decreed death for both himself and the Stanleys.

The easier way out would be to knock over Ferd and then escape in the dark on one of the four horses. He couldn't do it because it would forsake and doom the Stanleys. Not one but all four of these killers must somehow be dealt with and downed.

To deal with the first one Lindsay stepped abruptly around the cottonwood bole with his shotgun clubbed. He hit hard with it twice, smashing the barrel down on Ferd's head and battering him to the ground. To make sure of no outcry he struck a third time and a fourth, pounding hard on the man's skull.

With his heart thumping, Marcus Lindsay dragged the senseless man to nearby underbrush. He took a rope from one of the saddles and secured Ferd's hands and feet, then pushed him under a bush.

What next? Next, he reasoned, the man with the lantern might come this way in his hunt for the wagon driver. If so he could be clubbed down. If he didn't come, eventually he'd return to the wagon to report no success in the search. In which case, sooner or later, Plover would send one of his men here to check with Ferd or perhaps to saddle the four Stanley horses for the final getaway.

One thing at a time, Lindsay decided as he crouched behind the big tree to await whoever or whatever might come.

What came, after a long wait, was a man with a lantern. "Ferd," the man called as he approached through the grove.

When he passed close by, Lindsay again stepped out from his shelter and hit hard with the clubbed shotgun. The man collapsed without an outcry.

Another saddle rope served to tie wrists and ankles. Lindsay drew the knots taut, then left the man bound and senseless under the bush with Ferd. From each he took a forty-five gun and stuck them in his own belt.

Now he'd have something to shoot with even if he emptied the shotgun.

But the shotgun was still his surest weapon against the two outlaws ransacking the Stanley wagon. As Lindsay moved that way through the trees a sound made him jump to one side, stumbling. It was only one of his own mules wandering back to join the horses.

Picking himself up, Lindsay moved on toward a glimmer of lantern light at the wagon. The scene there hadn't changed. The lumps of the two Stanleys on the ground—Warren stunned, Paul conscious but wounded. Four outlaw horses standing by. The covered wagon now stripped of its baggage, a lantern set eerily on its tongue.

And two men in ugly frustration searching for money that wasn't there.

At the moment they were about ten feet apart. Lindsay aimed his shotgun at Floyd Plover, then waited for the other man to move closer to Plover—close enough so that a few duckshot from the spread barrel would hit each man. The thought of killing brought a nausea to Lindsay and he decided to shoot low, thigh-high. It should put both outlaws out of the fight and . . .

From the down creek thicket came a shout of warning. The voice was Ferd's, who must have regained consciousness under a bush.

"Look out, Floyd! He's got a shotgun!"

Plover and the man with him each drew a gun, whirling toward Lindsay. One of them, the stocky man with a scarred forehead, came charging straight toward the sound of Ferd's voice which was also directly toward Lindsay.

At ten yards he saw the shape of Lindsay crouching in the gloom of the grove with the shotgun. Floyd Plover fired twice at that shape, yelling: "Here he is, Frank! Get him."

And Marcus Lindsay, nameless wanderer who never before had shot at anything but wild game, squeezed both of his triggers. He aimed neither high nor low, merely let fly convulsively with both barrels at the man with the blazing gun who charged headlong toward him.

Plover, long-wanted Idaho outlaw, fell riddled

with duckshot. As he fell the man at the wagon made a dive for the nearest horse. He jumped into its saddle and the night swallowed him as he raced off, leaving Lindsay too paralyzed with the shock of his own victory to shoot again.

Presently Lindsay moved to a water bucket and soaked a rag in it. The cold, wet touch brought Warren to his senses. The man stared vacantly, "Where are they, John?"

"One got away. This one didn't." Lindsay motioned toward the sprawled body of Plover.

Paul, who'd never quite lost consciousness, spoke huskily. "He licked them, Warren. Licked them all by himself."

Warren got up unsteadily to give first aid to his brother. The wound was in Paul's shoulder and might fester. "We better make a fire and heat some water, John. There's a bandage kit in the wagon." Then Warren Stanley's brain cleared and he remembered. "There were four of them. What happened to the other two?"

"I'll fetch them," Lindsay said.

He went first to the wagon, found a box of shells and reloaded the shotgun. From under the wagon seat he took a kit containing turpentine and bandages. After handing it to Warren he hurried down creek through the grove.

When he came back he was marching two prisoners in front of him. He'd untied their ankles but their wrists were still bound. Walking behind them, Lindsay prodded them with the shotgun. The man called Ferd had a beanpole build and a bullet head. The other was middle-sized, middle-aged and chunky. The sight of Plover's body panicked them as they passed it on the way to the fire, which had just been kindled by Warren Stanley.

Lindsay made each prisoner sit with his back to a tree. He wound a lariat around each man and his tree and retied their feet. "It'll hold them till morning," he said.

Warren set a pail of water on the fire. The supper coffee pot was half full and he put it beside the pail. "Soon as I get Paul fixed up, John, I'll ride to Glenn's Ferry for help. We'd better grain one of the horses." He fixed a cold eye on the prisoners. "Who's Lew?" he demanded.

"Never heard of him," Ferd whined. The other outlaw echoed him.

It was Floyd Plover who'd mentioned the name Lew, and Plover was dead. So it was possible that only Plover could have answered questions about Lew.

"There was a Lew Rogan," Lindsay reminded Warren, "on the stage with your sister."

Warren bathed Paul's wound with hot water and applied turpentine. While he was bandaging the shoulder joint Lindsay told him about the Bliss Ranch strayman he'd met on the road. "We got

113

three of four stolen horses back for them, so they ought to be glad to lend us a hand. Paul won't be fit for the saddle for maybe a week."

"At Glenn's Ferry," Warren decided, "I'll arrange to send him to Boise City by buckboard. Nan can take care of him till we get there. Did the strayman tell you how big a place Glenn's Ferry is?"

"Yes, I asked about that. He said it's the most important crossing of the Snake for a hundred miles each way. It's got a ferry, a store, saloon, relay station, post office, livery barn and a deputy sheriff who looks after the east end of Owyhee County."

"Good." From a trail map Warren already knew that Owyhee, Idaho's most southwesterly county, was the largest in the territory. Its county seat, Silver City, lay a hundred miles west of Glenn's Ferry, the only settlement of importance in the eastern half of the county. "Let's hope they've got a doctor there, John."

Lindsay led the three outlaw horses down creek and picketed them with the others. He saddled one of the Stanley mounts for Warren's emergency ride to the ferry.

By then Warren had given Paul a drink of brandy and put him to bed in his blanket roll. Coffee was boiling and a pan of leftover stew was on the fire. "Better let me go instead of you," Lindsay offered.

"No. You tie these birds up tight and get some sleep. You sure earned it. Hadn't been for you we'd all be dead." He glanced toward Plover's body. "There'll be a coroner's inquest, maybe."

The word alarmed Lindsay. An inquest meant publicity in which he himself would be the central figure. It would put him in the limelight at Boise City. He remembered reading in the *Statesman* about the public reaction to Verne Hallam's rescue of the stagecoach. They'd made a hero out of Hallam. Important people like John Hailey and Milton Kelly had gone out of their way to applaud and befriend him.

And now, Marcus Lindsay saw with alarm, the same spotlight would shine on himself. He could imagine a cheering crowd waiting to meet the Stanley drive when it arrived at the capital. A crowd with Nan Stanley in it, eager to greet and thank a wagoneer called John Gresham who'd saved the lives and property of her brothers.

Would Lois Lindsay be there too? She seemed to have made a protégé of Nan.

It still lacked two hours of daybreak when Warren took to his saddle. The nine miles to Glenn's Ferry could easily be made in those two hours. "I'll be quick as I can, John." He gave spurs to his mount and was off. The deep ruts of the Overland Trail would guide him through the dark to Glenn's Ferry.

One of the prisoners whined a complaint. "You

115

gonna leave me hooked up like this all night?" He was the chunky, middle-aged man and for the first time Lindsay gave him a close inspection. "Your name wouldn't be Baker, would it? According to the papers, a guy with about your build suckered Verne Hallam to an empty house where friends of Plover beat him up."

"My name's Harper," the man said sullenly. "Gimme a slug of brandy."

Lindsay shook his head. "You're lucky you don't get the same kind of a slug you were fixing to give me." He took a tarp from the wagon and covered Plover's body.

After that he put more wood on the fire and tried to sleep. But a new and terrifying hazard kept him awake. Everything was different now. As an insignificant choreman on a farm eight miles from town he would hardly be noticed. But as a man who'd more than matched the feat of Verne Hallam, killing Floyd Plover and capturing single-handed two others of the gang, and putting a fourth to flight, all of Idaho would be wanting a look at John Gresham.

All of Idaho including Lois Lindsay—Lois with whom he must never come face to face! He might hide his identity from everyone else, Marcus Lindsay reasoned as he lay sleepless in the dark, but not from his own wife.

CHAPTER X

Rain beat on the barracks roof and outside the night was dark and muddy. Inside, all was gay and bright at a formal ball being given by the officers at Fort Boise. Verne Hallam, sitting by the wall with a stout army wife who'd danced herself out of breath, for the first time in his life was sorry he'd never learned to waltz. A square set he could manage, but not the round dances, which for most of the evening condemned him to sit by and watch Nan whirl past him first with one smartly-uniformed officer, then another. The cream of civilian society was there too, the ladies in low-cut gowns and the men in starched shirts. The russet-haired cowboy from Kansas made a marked contrast. Except for a gunbelt and a red bandana he was rigged out much as when Nan Stanley had first seen him at the Indian Creek hold-up.

He responded absently to chatter from the major's wife, who was telling him how much more resplendent these affairs had been at her husband's last post, Fort Laramie, Wyoming. "And so much more exciting, too, Mr. Hallam. I remember the Christmas ball thirteen years ago, in '66. At midnight we were all dancing, having a perfectly wonderful time, when Portugee Phillips burst in on us with news of the Fetterman massacre. Lieutenant Fetterman's entire party wiped out by four thousand Sioux under Red Cloud laying siege to Fort Phil Kearney!"

The lady gave a shudder and Verne said: "I reckon it broke up the party."

"Indeed it did. The bugle called 'Boots and Saddles' and our men went dashing off on a two-hundred-mile, zero-weather ride to Fort Kearney—Thank you, Lieutenant Patten. Now that I have my breath back, I'll be glad to."

Verne wasn't sorry when a junior officer led her out on the floor. Nan was dancing by with Captain Lovejoy and when the music stopped Verne saw them cross the room to join Mrs. Lindsay and Wade Canby at the punch bowl. Canby was having plenty of competition tonight. A dozen of Boise City's more eligible bachelors along with as many unattached officers were swarming around Lois. "Our last chance at you," a handsome captain named Borland had remarked earlier, "before Canby takes you out of circulation."

The fiddlers began another number for which Borland claimed Lois and Wade Canby danced away with Nan Stanley. Nan, radiant in a full-skirted dance frock of pale yellow, waved at Verne as she whirled by.

Maybe, Verne pondered, he'd been unfair to Canby. Important people like Colonels Green and

Bernard, Governor Biggerstaff and John Hailey all were on a basis of firm friendship with the engineer. The only score Verne could hold against him was the glimpse of Lew Rogan furtively slipping a note into Canby's pocket. Maybe there'd been an innocent reason for it. And after all there was no score against Rogan except that twelve years ago he'd been discharged as an Idaho City constable on suspicion of taking a bribe. Even if the suspicion had been justified, a man might reform in twelve years.

Jim Agnew, the capital's leading liveryman, spied Verne and came to sit by him. "How did those carriage lamps work, boy?"

"Fine," Verne said. "Without them we'd 've got lost in the dark."

Agnew's stable had furnished many of the carriages which had brought town couples out to the post. Because of the storm he'd equipped them with carriage lamps. Verne's main thrill had been the necessity of carrying Nan from the carriage to the barracks door to keep her dance pumps out of the mud.

"She looks kinda cute, don't she?" Agnew said as he followed Verne's gaze. "Did she hear from her brothers on the afternoon stage?"

Verne nodded. "She got a letter postmarked Salmon Falls. It said they'll write her again from Glenn's Ferry. Which reminds me: how come there's no telegraph wire along that stage road?

119

This being a territorial capital, with an army post, you'd think they'd have a wire to the railroad."

"They do," the liveryman said, "but it runs to Winnemucca, Nevada."

The Winnemucca route, he explained, was rougher but a little shorter. It ran southwest through Silver City to strike the transcontinental railroad about two hundred miles west of Kelton, Utah. "Freight from California comes via Winnemucca, and freight from the east comes via Kelton. A telegraph wire follows the Winnemucca road. A few years ago we had some bad Indian trouble on the Winnemucca road, but not lately."

"A lady," Verne remarked, "was just telling me about Indian trouble which broke up a dance one time—Look, isn't that Constable Paxton? Wonder what he's doing here."

"He's muddyin' up the floor, for one thing," Agnew said. "Looks kind of het up. And dogged if he ain't headin' straight for that gal of yours, boy."

Boise City's night constable, muddy boots and all, was tapping Nan Stanley on the arm. Her partner, Wade Canby, stopped and they both gave attention to what seemed to be sensational information. Lois and Captain Borland joined them. Nan, clearly alarmed, was asking quick questions.

Then both couples and Paxton himself hurried straight to Verne Hallam.

"You'll have to take me home, Verne," Nan said. "Paul just got here and he has a bullet wound."

"A Bliss Ranch cowboy," Paxton explained, "fetched him here in a buckboard from Glenn's Ferry. Along with two of the buggers who shot him. An Owyhee County deputy came along too. The Plover gang done it but they got the short end of a gunfight. Your other brother's okay, Miss." The constable spoke directly to Verne. "Marshal Robbins wants you at the jail, Hallam. Wants to see if you can identify the two prisoners."

Agnew got up briskly. "I'll have your carriage at the door in five minutes, boy."

"We'd better go too, Wade," Lois Lindsay decided. She and Nan went at once to an anteroom where they'd left their wraps.

Verne, standing with Canby, Paxton and Captain Borland, listened to a few more details. "The Plover gang," Paxton informed them, "somehow got the idea that the Stanley boys had five thousand in cash with them. It was a bum tip because the money was in a bank draft and they'd already mailed it to the bank here. But the gang thought they had it in cash and so they stuck up the Stanley camp nine miles the other side of Glenn's Ferry. Four of 'em hit 'em in the middle of the night when they were asleep."

Verne stared. "But you said they got the short end of it! How could four armed robbers get bested in a fight with three sleeping campers?"

Paxton grimaced. "Ask Paul Stanley. You won't believe it even when he tells you. Paul was shot cold right off the bat. Warren was knocked over and tied up just as fast. But the teamster—some tramp mule skinner named Gresham—had gone to bed with a shotgun. And believe it or not, all by himself he filled Floyd Plover full of duckshot, captured two others and made the fourth take off on a horse. Damnedest thing you ever heard of. Wait till you hear Paul tell about it!"

It was still raining when two carriages drew up at the barracks doorway. Again Verne carried Nan Stanley three steps and put her on a rear seat, where he drew curtains to keep out the rain. This time he let Agnew's coachman drive them. As they left the parade ground, wheels splashed through puddles and flicked up lumps of mud. The roadway was still a mire when they turned into Warm Springs Avenue. Looking back, Verne saw the shape of Canby's carriage as he followed with Mrs. Lindsay.

"Did the constable tell you anything else?" Nan asked.

"Only that four wide-awake outlaws went up against three sleeping campers and got the worst of it. Thanks to a one-man army named Gresham."

"They found a deputy sheriff at Glenn's Ferry?"

"Yes, a young Owyhee County deputy who's stationed there. He brought along the two prisoners and tomorrow he'll take 'em down to Silver City on the Winnemucca stage. They'll have to be tried there because it's the county seat of Owyhee." After another look back Verne said, "Canby's turning in at the Lindsay driveway."

Nan nodded. "She told me in the cloakroom she'd go straight home and then have Mr. Canby join us at the Overland. He's to tell her if there's any way she can help."

The rain had slackened to a drizzle when the carriage stopped at the Overland Hotel. Here there was a high board walk and Nan raised her skirts to scurry across it. Verne followed her into the lobby where the night clerk didn't wait for her question.

"Your brother's in 208, Miss Stanley. Doc Eph Smith is with him."

Nan raced up the stairs and by the time Verne overtook her she was bending over Paul's bed. Of two men standing by, one was Eph Smith and the other wore the trappings of a cowboy.

"I'm feelin' fine, Sis," Paul said after she'd kissed him. "Only reason they had to put me to bed was that the ride from Glenn's Ferry jolted me some."

The girl looked inquiringly at Doctor Smith, who reassured her. "The bullet missed the shoulder bone and left only a flesh wound. The

Glenn's Ferry people did a good job on it."

A swarthy cowboy by the bed said: "I didn't want to lose no time, Miss, so I changed teams twice and pushed right through. A deputy and two prisoners came along with us. Gunther's my name and I ride for the Bliss outfit on Snake River."

"The Bliss Ranch did a lot for us," Paul said. "They loaned Warren a rider to help him get the cattle nine miles farther on to Glenn's Ferry, then let Gunther take me on to Boise."

"Least we could do," Gunther said, "after your outfit got back three stolen horses for us and gunned down the gang that stole 'em."

"It was John Gresham did that," Paul insisted, "all by himself. Hadn't been for Gresham, Warren and I'd be pushing up daisies."

Eph Smith picked up his satchel. "I'll give you just ten minutes with him, folks. Then you must clear out and let him get some rest."

When he was gone Paul gave Nan a newspaper clipping. "It's an ad for a section of fenced land eight miles down the valley from here. For sale or lease. Warren and I think it could be just what we're looking for. We want it checked right away. If we like it, and can make a deal, we could take the cows straight there and not have to cross the Boise River."

Nan read the ad aloud to Verne. "Six-room house and good cottonwood shade!" she repeated with a glow of excitement. "I'm dying to see it, Paul."

"Which is exactly what Warren wants you to do. And right away. Tomorrow. The doc won't let me go so you'll have to tend to it yourself. First, see Mr. Huntoon at the bank and get a lease price on it. If it's reasonable, hire a livery rig and a guide and go down there for a look. See if you'd like to live there, Nan."

"I'll drive her myself," Verne offered. "How about it?"

"It's a date," Nan agreed. "I'll have to see the banker first, to get the key."

Paul looked at Verne with a shrewd approval. "Warren and I read about you in the paper, fella. About your chasing away those road agents from Nan's stage. Thanks plenty."

"It was a tame show," Verne said with a grin, "compared to the one that wagon man of yours put on. I'd sure like to meet that guy."

"And I too," Nan echoed warmly.

"You will," Paul assured them, "because we've talked him into working for us permanent. He'll do the chores and teaming work for us at the ranch. But you won't like the looks of him, Nan. He was in a bad accident one time and has burn scars all over his face and head. The first time you see him you'll want to look the other way."

"No I won't," the girl said. "After what he's done for us I'll love him on sight. Come on,

Verne. You too, Mr. Gunther. Our ten minutes are up." She kissed Paul goodnight and blew out the lamp.

Verne and the Bliss hand left her at the door of her room and went down to the lobby. Wade Canby was just coming in on his way up to see Paul Stanley.

"You're too late," Verne told him. "He's tucked in for the night. Nothing left to do now except for me to identify a couple of prisoners."

"I'll tag along," Gunther decided. "Want to see Chuck Prather before he takes off for Silver City in the morning."

"I'm kinda curious about those birds myself," Canby said. He went out with the two cowboys and the three walked in a light drizzle to the jail.

Marshal Robbins and the Owyhee County deputy were waiting there. The deputy, Chuck Prather, had a boyish, beardless face and looked barely more than twenty-one years old. Robbins thumbed toward the cell block. "They're in the first cage on the right, Hallam. Take a look."

A quick look was all Verne needed. "The tall skinny guy," he said as he rejoined Robbins, "was one of the Indian Creek stage robbers. I had a peek at him without his mask, remember? The chunky man's the one who woke me up at three in the morning and conned me down to a house on Grove Street. Called himself Baker. He just took me to the gate, then he let me go in by

126

myself and get beat up. Did you look to see if the tall skinny guy's got a bullet scar on his arm?"

"We did. No scar."

"I winged one of those three stage robbers. So the man I winged must be the one who made a getaway from the Stanley trail camp."

"That's the way I figure it," Robbins agreed.

The youthful Glenn's Ferry deputy, Prather, remembered something. "I forgot to tell you, Marshal. The teamster Gresham heard Floyd Plover use a name while he was sticking up the camp. He asked the Stanleys where they kept their five thousand dollars. Warren said, 'In a bank.' And Plover said, 'Yeah? Either you're a liar or Lew is.' Sounded like they had a tip from somebody named Lew that the outfit had five thousand in cash."

It seemed to Verne that he heard a faint catching of breath behind him. If so, Wade Canby quickly recovered himself. His face was in repose when Verne turned to look.

Orlando Robbins gazed shrewdly at Chuck Prather. "Humph! Two ways to spell that name. L-o-u or L-e-w. Lots of Lous on this range. One time I jailed a Lou Bixby for stealing a sheep."

"What puts teeth in it," Prather said, "is that the Stanley boys actually *did* leave Kelton with five thousand dollars. Only it was in a bank draft and somewhere along the trail they forwarded it to the Boise City bank for deposit."

"We'll work on it, Chuck. Better get some sleep, boy. Your prisoners'll be ready for you in the morning, when the Winnemucca stage pulls out."

"Sorry I can't hang around," the young deputy said, "until the Stanley drive gets here. If I know this town they'll turn out the Capital band for that mule skinner, Gresham."

"He's got it coming," Robbins agreed generously.

Wade Canby glanced at a wall clock. "Gosh! It's long after midnight. Guess I'll go turn in. See you tomorrow, men."

The abruptness of his departure made Verne thoughtful. If the man had a shady connection with Lew Rogan he'd be on pins and needles to warn Rogan about Plover's mention of the name Lew. Rogan had ridden the stage from Kelton with Nan Stanley and during the fifty-hour journey he might have heard her tell of five thousand dollars her brothers were bringing along to start an Idaho ranch.

If there was a link between Rogan and the Plover gang their tip could easily have come from Rogan. Was Canby now on his way to warn the man?

"Time I'm turning in too," Verne said. He went quickly out and saw Canby turn east at the Idaho Street corner. With his coat collar turned up against the drizzle Verne hurried that way to keep him in sight.

It wasn't difficult because Canby only went as far as Seventh Street where he entered the Central Hotel. Since the man kept a permanent room at the Central he was probably going to bed after all.

Unless . . . ! A possibility made Verne go into the Central lobby. By then Canby had taken his room key from a rack and disappeared upstairs. There was no night clerk, merely a bell whose button an incomer could press for service.

Verne went to the registry book and turned to a page which listed the permanent roomers. Canby's name was on it. His room was 218. The last name on the pay-by-the-week list was Lew Rogan, whose room was 230.

So Canby could contact the man right here. He'd need merely to walk down a corridor half a dozen doors from his own. This very minute he could be warning Rogan about the use of his name by Plover.

Verne moved quietly up the stairs. The upper hallway had a dim lamplight and by it he found door number 218. The transom told him that the room was dark. If Canby had entered to go to bed he would hardly undress without a light.

To make sure, Verne tapped on the door. There was no response. It meant that Wade Canby had gone to some room other than his own.

Room 230 was on the same side of the corridor and six doors away. Verne went to it and its transom showed that a lamp was lighted inside. Putting an ear to the door he could hear subdued voices. Was it Canby warning Rogan?

By walking in on them he could find out. For a convincing excuse he could suggest that Rogan himself go to the jail and confirm the identification of the tall, thin robber. Rogan had been present at the stage hold-up and although he'd seen no unmasked faces he could at least remember the man's build and perhaps his voice. And since the prisoners would leave early in the morning for Silver City, any local inspection of them would need to be made tonight.

With that cover-up in mind Verne Hallam rapped on the door.

From inside came breathless silence. No-one answered. A second knock still brought no response.

With his third rapping Verne called out, "Are you up, Rogan?"

This time the door opened and Rogan stood there in his night shirt, his fleshy face slyly apprehensive. No-one was in the room with him. The room had a closet but its door stood wide open to show that no-one was hiding there.

But the window was also open and it gave to a narrow balcony which extended along the hotel's Idaho Street side. The window in room 218 would give to that same balcony.

The visitor's means of retreat was so obvious

that Verne didn't bother to offer his trumped-up excuse for the intrusion. "I see I'm too late," he said with a fixed stare at the open window. "It's a rainy night so you'd better close it."

He went back down the hall and as he passed door number 218 he could tell by the transom that the room was still unlighted. But the stealthy dropping of a shoe meant that Wade Canby was undressing in the dark.

CHAPTER XI

Verne tied a livery rig at the Overland hitchrack and went into the lobby hoping to find Nan there. It was a little past nine in the morning. "Miss Stanley isn't back from the bank yet," the clerk said. "Her brother wants to see you in 208."

Verne found Paul propped up in bed reading today's *Statesman*. "Nothing about the raid on our camp," he said. "The news didn't get here in time. Did Chuck Prather get off with his prisoners?"

"Bright and early," Verne told him. "They say it's a sixty-mile run to Silver City on a rough road. Take 'em all day to get there. What about the dead man? Floyd Plover? Did they bury him at Glenn's Ferry?"

"Had to. But Warren and I and Gunther and Prather and John Gresham all signed a report of what happened, and Chuck Prather's taking it to the Silver City coroner. Quite a responsibility for that deputy, herding those two outlaws down there. He's barely more than a kid."

Verne had decided not to mention Wade Canby's pussy-footing call on Rogan the night before until he could back it up with solid proof. Canby was an established and popular citizen here in town and his word would carry more

132

weight than Hallam's. The man's call at Rogan's room couldn't be indisputably proved. Even if proved, Canby could assign to it some reason entirely unconnected with the crimes of Floyd Plover.

"You could do us one more favor, Hallam, if you will," Paul Stanley said. "But maybe it's too much to ask."

"Name it."

"With me laid up here, Warren needs an extra hand to help him push three hundred cows up the Overland road. The Bliss outfit helped him get them as far as Glenn's Ferry and they're resting on riverbank grass there. But it's still ninety-odd miles to Boise City, a week's drive. If you could . . ."

"I'll start early in the morning," Verne broke in with a grin.

"How good of you!" Nan exclaimed from the doorway. She'd just returned from the bank with a key in her hand. "I won't worry about Warren any more now."

"Is that the key to the ranch house?" Paul asked her.

"Yes. The bank says it's an estate they're closing out. The owner, an Abner Brown, died and his heirs back east don't want to run it. They'll lease for one thousand-a-year with an option to buy for ten thousand cash."

"Sounds okay, Sis. You and Hallam run along

and take a look at it. Find out if there's any adjacent government land that Warren and I could file on. Did the bank get our draft?"

"It's on deposit for us and here's the bank book." Nan laid a tiny credit book on the table, kissed her brother goodbye, took Verne's arm and went gayly out on the tour of inspection.

The ferry at the foot of Seventh carried them across the Boise River. Just beyond the river Verne left the stage road and turned west down the riverbank along the moist ruts of a wagon road. Jim Agnew had told him how to find the Abner Brown place. The air was balmy after last night's rain. A belt of cottonwood timber flanked the river and jaybirds scolded from the branches.

For the first mile Verne kept his team at an easy trot, then a series of muddy spots slowed him to a walk. They passed a small dairy farm from which the trees had been cleared. All the while Nan chattered about the unknown which lay ahead—the house which might become her future home. Verne made only a few responses and at last she sensed his preoccupation.

"Something's troubling you, Verne. Do you want to tell me about it?"

He felt an urge to confide his suspicions about Canby. Yet there were reasons not to. While he hesitated, a rifle barked from the trees about a hundred yards to the left and Verne saw a squirrel tumble from a high branch to the ground. A homespun farm hand appeared with a rifle and picked it up.

"Goodness!" Nan exclaimed. "That hunter didn't even see us!"

"We didn't see *him* either—until after he fired."

It put Verne in a mood of sober caution. Allies of the Plover gang had tried to kill him in the Grove Street house. If his suspicions about Rogan were right, they'd have more reason than ever now. And plenty of opportunity. That harmless hunter might just as easily have been a killer in ambush, dispatched by Rogan or Canby to waylay Hallam in a lonely woods.

If he confided in Nan, she'd know as much about Rogan and Canby as he knew himself. Which meant that she'd share the same jeopardy. Two shots, as easily as one, could be fired at a buggy in the woods.

"You haven't answered my question," Nan said.

"I'm thinking about that game teamster, Gresham," Verne said. And indirectly he was. For allies of the Plover gang had even more of a score to settle with John Gresham. He'd shotgunned their leader and turned two of them over to the law. "Those crooks won't sleep good till they get him. They could sneak up on him any night in camp."

"But only one of them's left now."

"Only one of them got away from the camp

135

raid," Verne admitted. "But the two who socked me in an empty house are still on the loose. We don't know how many more are hooked up with them. For instance the guy who tipped 'em off about the five thousand dollars."

"Two of them, thank goodness, are on their way to jail at Silver City."

"Jailbirds have been known to fly away," Verne said.

For four miles below the ferry the road followed close to the river. Then a farm fence forced the road to leave the timbered bottomland and follow a bare bench prairie for the next several miles. Verne's rig flushed a pair of sage hens and scattered a bunch of grazing range mares. Beyond another fence a shabby, shadeless shack and tumbledown barn made up the improvements of a farm and brought a discouraged look to Nan. "Let's hope the Brown place isn't like that."

It wasn't, and Verne knew it the instant he sighted the gate. The gate was painted white and had the name Abner Brown over it. A four-wire fence had good cedar posts. In the distance beyond, a shingled house roof and a barn roof of sheet iron showed against the green of cottonwood trees. A patch of lighter green marked a meadow.

"Looks like it's pretty well kept up," Verne said as he drove through the gate.

Nan's cheeks were bright with excited anticipation as they moved on to the house. It was one-and-a-half stories with dormer windows. Around it a picket fence enclosed a weed-grown yard. Stalks of hollyhocks not yet in bloom peeped over the weeds.

There was a hay barn, a corral and several sheds, with a pulley well in the barnyard. The house faced the open bench prairie but a grove of river bottom cottonwoods came almost to the back door. "A man could start a right good cow outfit here," Verne said. He'd inquired of Agnew and learned that the prairie side of the section was still unfiled on. If each of the Stanley brothers filed a homestead adjacent to the south fence, they could control in all a section and a half of land.

Verne took Nan through the picket gate and walked her through knee-deep weeds to the house. Her key fit the door and inside they found dusty pine floors. The place had been vacant since winter and there were cobwebs. The windows had blinds but no curtains. There was a fireplace with a pine board mantel over it. In spite of the shabby emptiness Nan looked around her entranced. "I can make it beautiful!" she exclaimed.

"I'll check the outsheds," Verne said, and left her there.

He went out and explored a six-stall barn with a grain bin and a vestibule with racks for saddles and harness. Each stall had a manger with a loft hole over it. The rear of the barn aisle gave on a spruce-pole corral across a corner of which ran a small, dry ditch.

The ditch was important and Verne followed it around the upper edge of a twenty-acre timothy meadow. There'd been no-one here to irrigate and so the crop, though green, would hardly be worth cutting this season. Above the meadow the ditch angled not toward the Boise River but to a small tributary creek coming in from the south. Did it have a diversion dam and headgate? Paul Stanley would ask about that and so Verne walked the length of the ditch to where it came out of willows along the creeklet.

There was a diversion dam and headgate but the creek itself was dry. Irrigation water would come only during melting snow or heavy summer rains.

Verne went back to the barnyard and was about to rejoin Nan at the house when he saw a distant rider approaching from the direction of Boise City. The rider wore a gunbelt and his saddle scabbard had a rifle. Had a killer followed him here? Verne wondered. It could be one of the pair who'd jumped him in the Grove Street house. Maybe the man with the round, red-stubbled face!

Verne checked the loads in his six-gun, then stood just inside the barn vestibule. In the open he'd be at a disadvantage because the other man had a rifle.

But as the rider came nearer Verne relaxed. He grinned sheepishly as the man dismounted at the barn. "Hello, Gunther. What brings *you* out here?"

"Paul Stanley tells me you're riding to Glenn's Ferry tomororw," the Bliss cowboy said, "to help his brother bring on the cattle."

"That's right. Bright and early tomorrow."

"Then why not ride back with me? We could tie your saddle horse behind my buckboard."

"Why not?" Verne agreed. Gunther had driven Paul Stanley to Boise City in a private conveyance, Deputy Chuck Prather bringing along the two hand-cuffed prisoners in the same rig. The rig must now be returned to the Glenn's Ferry liveryman. But it didn't explain why Gunther had just ridden eight miles to this valley farm.

When Verne asked bluntly for a reason, the Glenn's Ferry cowboy gave it. "Truth is Orlando Robbins got worried and asked me to side you. He couldn't come himself because he and a batch of deputies are riding hell-bent to a place they call Massacre Canyon."

"Where's that?" Verne asked with a vacant stare. He didn't see Nan come out of the house and walk toward the barn.

"It's on the stage road to Silver City and about halfway there," Gunther said. "That road crosses the Snake River at Mundy's Ferry right where Reynolds Creek comes in from the other side.

Reynolds Creek comes down a rocky canyon with a plumb bad reputation. More stagecoaches've been held up there than any other place in Idaho."

Nan's voice surprised them. "Yes, Mrs. Lindsay was telling me about that place." The girl had approached unnoticed and stood just beyond Gunther's horse.

Gunther saw her and took off his hat. "There's plenty to tell about it, Miss. Back in '67 and '68 a band of renegade Snake Indians used to swarm down on stages and freight wagons going through that canyon. Later it got to be a favorite spot for road agents who wanted to stick up bullion shipments on the way to Winnemucca. You could make a first-class graveyard out of folks that've been killed there."

Verne asked: "You mean Robbins just got word of another hold-up there?"

Gunther shook his head. "Not yet—and let's hope he won't. But about two hours ago he found out that three mean-looking riders, leading two saddled horses, were seen fording the Boise River about daybreak. One of those riders had a round, red-stubbled face. The other two are hard cases who've been known to hang around Dutch Henry's bar. They left Boise City about an hour ahead of the Silver City stage and on the same road."

That would be the coach on which the boyish deputy named Prather was taking the two outlaw prisoners to the Owyhee County jail. "So maybe," Verne said, "they figure to waylay the stage and rescue a couple of pals!"

"It's a fair bet, Hallam. Else why would they be leading two saddled horses? Trouble is Robbins heard about it too late. The three men left at five. The stage left at six. And Robbins didn't get started till ten. He can't make Reynolds Creek Canyon before two in the afternoon. And the stage for Silver City's due there about noon."

"But what's that got to do with your riding out here?"

"Robbins says it won't hurt to check on you too. So here I am." Gunther relaxed and rolled a cigaret. "Mighty glad to see that everything's all right."

"Everything's perfect," Nan exclaimed. "I'd love living here, Verne. You must help me persuade Paul."

She took him to the house and on a tour through it. The two upper rooms had low, sloping ceilings and dormer windows. "We can let our choreman have one of them," she planned. "That nice Mr. Gresham who saved everything for us. We'll paint the walls and put matting on the floors. The minute Paul says yes I'll start making curtains."

Verne smiled dryly. "The house is only on one acre. The other six hundred and thirty-nine acres aren't bad, either."

The tour continued outside and through a shady

grove back of the house. All the while Verne's mind fastened on the three outlaws who'd crossed to this side of the river leading two saddled horses. There was a missing motive somewhere. Was Gunther holding back something?

While Nan inspected an outshed which the Abner Browns had used for a poultry house Verne had a chance to question Gunther out of her hearing.

"The marshal figured it like this," Gunther explained. "His best bet is that those buggers aim to stick up the stage. But he can't overlook a long shot either. That's why he sent me foggin' along after you and the girl."

"If they wanted to drygulch me," Verne argued, "they wouldn't bring along two extra horses."

"Look. Four people can identify 'em in court. The Stanley brothers and John Gresham for the camp raid, you for the Indian Creek and Grove Street jobs. Right?"

"Right. So what?"

"So what would be the best way for 'em to shut those four witnesses up?"

"They'd have to kill us off."

"Which they can't do. Paul's safe in a hotel room. Warren and Gresham are ninety miles away at Glenn's Ferry. Which leaves only you. If they drygulch you, it still leaves three to nail 'em in court. But suppose they gang up on you today as you drive the girl to this farm and back along

142

a lonely riverbank? Say they nab you both and put you on the two extra horses! And take you both to some hideout in the hills? And then send word to the Stanleys to keep their mouths shut, or else!"

It was indeed a long shot but it could explain the two extra horses. Those extra saddles might be used either in a rescue or kidnapping operation. "We'll keep our eyes open on our way back to town," Verne said.

"And our guns limber."

On the return trip upriver the Bliss cowboy rode alertly at the wheel of Verne's rig. Listening absently to Nan's chatter Verne kept an equally sharp watch.

Nothing happened. The few people encountered were all friendly valley farmers. A ferry took them across the Boise River and they drove at a trot up Seventh to Main. When Verne let Nan out at the Overland Hotel she rushed upstairs to tell Paul about the Abner Brown ranch.

After getting rid of his rig Verne went to supper with Gunther at the Palace Restaurant. Jim Agnew joined them there with a pioneer blacksmith named Tom Maupin. Later the four went next door to a bar where the three older men traded treats while Verne smoked one of Agnew's cheroots and listened to their talk. Maupin regaled them with tales of the gold boom days of the Sixties. "Those were wild and woolly times," he remembered. "More gold dust came into this town than you could shake a stick at and some of it was bogus. A gunplay or two nearly every night, both here and at Idaho City."

"What about Silver City?"

"Bullion rollin' out of there every day for Winnemucca, on Wells Fargo coaches. Lot of Indian trouble down that way too. There was an ornery band of Snake Indians who used to raise hell along Reynolds Creek Canyon. That's half way to Silver City on the stage road. Like the raid in March of '67 when Bill Younger's stage got hit and all four of his passengers scalped. Same thing happened to Fred Jarvis's freight outfit at the same spot. Then there was . . . !"

"There was today!" a voice from the doorway interrupted. Ben Alanson, one of Sheriff Oldham's deputies, stood there with bad news on his face. "And at that same spot. Only this time it wasn't Indians. It was three white devils hiding behind rocks in Massacre Canyon. They shot up the Silver City stage, killed the driver and all his passengers except two."

The men at the bar stared. "Which two?" Agnew asked hoarsely.

"The two prisoners Chuck Prather was hauling to the Owyhee County jail. The raiders had saddled horses all ready for them. Orlando Robbins got there three hours too late and he just sent back word about it. Said accordin' to the hoofmarks the five of 'em took off east toward a fork of the Bruneau."

Tom Maupin swore under his breath.

Jim Agnew downed his liquor and looked at the cowboy from Kansas. "They're poison, that outfit. Next time they'll be after *you,* Hallam."

"Never mind *me,*" Verne said. He was thinking of Chuck Prather, the deputy sheriff no older than himself. Did he have a family? Verne wondered.

CHAPTER XII

At the next sunrise Wade Canby rode north out of Boise City, heading up Cottonwood Gulch on the Idaho City stage road. His mount was a strong, long-gaited sorrel, faster than most, but it would take him till nearly sunset to cover the thirty-five miles to the once booming gold town of Idaho City.

"They want me to appraise an old property, up there," had been his excuse when asking a livery hostler to saddle up for him.

The same hostler had just finished saddling a roan for Verne Hallam. From across Eighth Street Wade Canby had watched Hallam tie the mount to the endgate of a buckboard and drive off toward Glenn's Ferry with a cowboy named Gunther. Gunther had to return the rig to its owner and Hallam was on his way to help with the Stanley cattle drive.

He, Canby, had kept well out of Hallam's sight, leery of him after the escape the night before last from Rogan's room. Chances were ten to one that Hallam had seen enough, or heard enough, to guess the truth—that Rogan's furtive visitor was Canby himself, who'd slipped along a balcony to his own room.

If so it meant that Hallam was almost as

dangerous a threat as was Marcus Lindsay. For Hallam had somehow connected him with Rogan, and Rogan, if not a known rogue, at least had a cloud over his past. If Hallam should accuse him of conspiring with Rogan it would embarrass him with Lois Lindsay and not be easy to explain. The wedding date was less than a month away now. Nothing must be allowed to stand in the way of it. Lois herself, even without her fortune, was a priceless prize.

Canby pushed on up the twists of Cottonwood Gulch whose small stream was made muddy by Chinese placer miners panning gravel. Very little gold dust was left after fifteen years of pannings, but a few dollars a day was enough to keep a Chinese miner industriously at it. Hillsides along the gulch were treeless and brown.

Toward its head the gulch steepened and eight miles out of Boise City Canby reached a pass on a shoulder of Shaw's Mountain. He could hear the bump-rumpitty-thump of Plowman's quartz mill and saw a chain of carts hauling ore from the Rising Sun and Paymaster mines. In all of Ada County these were the only two lode mines still producing at a profit.

From here the road dipped into a gulch thickly timbered with conifers and through them Canby glimpsed a big overshot wheel turned by the waters of Robie Creek. That stream took him to a fork of More's Creek and the trail followed down it to a larger fork coming in from the north. Canby turned his sorrel up this main fork, and up a narrowing, fir-clad canyon. He'd now passed from Ada into Boise County, of which Idaho City was still the seat.

Near midday he met the stagecoach which ran daily from Idaho City to Boise City. A few miles farther on Canby met an ox-drawn wagon returning with a load of spruce poles after having delivered store goods to Pioneerville.

Others who saw him passed Wade Canby with greetings. It didn't matter, since none of them could possibly suspect the real reason for today's excursion.

In midafternoon he came to the mouth of Buzzard Gulch and as always it gave him a creepy feeling. For there he could see an old one-room cabin about fifty yards back from the road and almost hidden among the pines. The log cabin with the rusty iron roof where Canby, twelve years ago, had come within an eyelash of being trapped by vigilantes.

He'd ridden down from Idaho City with his saddle bags full of bogus dust intending to meet a messenger from the Pickett Corral gang here. He hadn't known that only a few days earlier all but one of the Pickett Corral gang had been shot or hung at Wahoe Ferry, and that the one had purchased his life by betraying the source of supply.

Just in the nick of time Wade Canby, after stopping his horse here, had seen a face peering from behind a tree. The face of a vigilante named Earnshaw. So he'd kept in his saddle and ridden on. Even now his neck could feel a twinge every time he thought of it. They'd given the would-be betrayer, he'd learned later, twenty-four hours to get out of Idaho and the man, one Gabe Henry, had never been seen since.

Canby spurred on and presently the country opened into a circular basin several miles in diameter and surrounded by magnificent pineclad mountains. The main fork of More's Creek cut through the middle of it with mounds of gravel along its banks where placer miners had reaped rich rewards for many years. A few were still there, panning for leftover dust, but the halcyon days were gone.

It was the same in Idaho City itself, not yet a ghost town but doomed to become one. What passed for a county courthouse was still there, and a sheriff's office, a shabby frame hotel and livery barn. There were two general stores still in business and three run-down saloons. Miners and prospectors from upper Grimes Creek and from high country around Pioneerville still came down for Saturday night revels.

Canby left his horse at the livery barn and crossed to Emery's bar where whisky was two bits a drink and information was free. "Did Old

Man Bascomb leave a message for me, Emery?" he asked.

"Ain't seen Bascomb for a coon's age, Mr. Canby. Have a drink."

Canby had one but insisted on paying for it. He called at another saloon and at both the stores, asking the same question and getting the same answer. It was all to create the illusion that he was here to appraise the old Bascomb mine.

On the way to the third saloon, Belle Plover's place, he passed the now-tumbledown house which had once served him as both residence and office. He could never forget his moment of panic when Constable Lew Rogan had come in with a search warrant. The eighty ounces of bogus gold dust he had on hand, if reported, would have put him in prison for many years—even if he were lucky enough to escape the wrath of the vigilantes. In those days bogus passers were fair game for lynchers all over Idaho.

The sly, greedy look in Rogan's eyes had saved Canby. His offer of a fat cash bribe had been accepted and the crisis was over. Soon after that Canby had moved his office to Boise City.

Belle Plover's place had once been the town's leading dance hall. Now it was only a third-rate bar with tarnished brass lamps, a cracked mirror and a sawdust floor. The only customers just now were a quartet of miners playing Seven Up, while Belle herself, a slattern in middle age, brought them mugs of beer. "Have you seen Old Man Bascomb lately?" Canby asked her.

She hadn't, of course. But Canby's next question told her he wanted to see her alone. "You showed me a collection of ore samples one time. Mind if I look at it again?"

It was a tradition in Idaho City for every saloon to display ore samples on tables and shelves around the barroom. In the past it had drawn trade. Canby knew that Belle Plover, born Belle Henry, kept hers in what had been a card room at the rear.

"Help yourself." She nodded in that direction. Canby stopped first at the bar where a Chinese bartender served him what tasted like moonshine whisky. Then he went back into the card room. A dusty table there was piled with chunks of quartz—low grade ore at which the engineer barely glanced.

He waited for Belle Plover and presently she came to him. "What's on your mind?" she asked curiously. "A gyp game of some kind, I bet."

"It's about your late husband. Can we have a little privacy?"

The woman stared for a moment, then led him to living quarters still further in the rear. There was a small sitting room and Canby sat down in a rocker. Belle remained standing.

"I just got the news about Floyd," she said. "It came on the stage yesterday. Somebody

151

shotgunned him down near Glenn's Ferry."

"How'd you like to get even?" Canby asked bluntly. "I mean with the man who killed your husband."

Belle's answer was quick and bitter. "I'd pull the trigger myself, if I could catch up with him."

"Trigger-pulling's a man's job, Belle. What about your brother Dutch, who tends bar in China Alley?"

Belle scoffed at it. "Dutch is too soft for a job like that. He ain't good for nothing except bar-swabbing."

"What about your brother Gabe? Got any idea where he is?"

"No. Nobody's seen hide nor hair of Gabe for twelve years."

Canby nodded. "Not since he saved his neck by steering vigilantes to the Buzzard Gulch cabin."

The woman didn't deny it. Instead she took a flask from a cabinet and poured two drinks. Canby could remember when she'd been not unattractive but now her cheeks were flabby, her tawny hair faded and unkempt. "You still holdin' that against him?" she asked as she passed a drink to Canby. She herself, with a bar in Idaho City and a brother in the Pickett Corral gang, had in the old days sometimes acted as a link between the supplier and the passers.

Canby answered her without rancor. "No. But

152

I figure the Henry family owes me something just the same. One of your brothers tried to trade my neck for his own. Now I want another of the Henry boys to make it up to me. You've got a third brother, Gil Henry. There's a Montana murder warrant out for him and he was seen crossing into Idaho. It's a fair bet he's hiding in the hills somewhere."

A secretive look came into Belle's pale moist eyes. "Hiding in what hills?"

"I don't know," Canby admitted. "But I'll wager that you do. Chances are he's not ten miles from where we are right now. There's a hundred deserted mine shacks in the woods around this basin. Somebody has to sneak grub to him and nobody'd do that but his loving sister. He's the baby of the family and he always was your pet, Belle. How often do you see him?"

"It's none of your damned business."

"Business! That's the right word, Belle. Because I'm offering you a straight business deal. How'd you like to have twelve thousand in cash? You and Gil. With a stake like that you could pull out of this rat-hole and go to Mexico or Peru. You and Gil could live easy down there."

The secretive look turned into a hard, calculating stare. "Twelve thousand in cash?"

"That plus revenge for the killing of your husband. The man who triggered the shotgun goes by the name of Gresham. John Gresham. It happens he's in my way. I can tell you where he is and you can pass the word to Gil."

"Gresham!" the woman brooded. "Yes, that's who the papers say done it. A teamster for some trail outfit. Where is he now?"

"For the next week he'll be on the Overland road moving about thirteen miles a day from Glenn's Ferry to Boise City. After that, if he's still alive, he'll be choreman at the Abner Brown farm eight miles downriver from Boise. Tell Gil he can pick his time and spot—but the quicker the better. You get the ten thousand in cash whenever Gil nails him."

"Ten? You said twelve."

"Sleeping right near him at those trail camps will be a cowboy named Hallam. You owe Hallam a slug too, for spoiling one of Floyd's road jobs a couple of weeks ago. Gil can slip up on a dark night and use two bullets as easy as one. The extra two thousand is for Hallam."

Belle Henry Plover eyed him sharply. "How do we know you'll pay?"

"I'd be scared not to, wouldn't I? If I welshed you could talk me into trouble."

"Maybe, and maybe not. If I told tales you'd deny 'em. And who'd they believe? It'd be the word of a busted saloon woman against the word of a high-flyer like you."

"It could put the skids under me just the same," Canby argued. "If you read the papers you know

154

I'm due to marry a rich woman next month. I wouldn't risk any scandal mess, would I, that might make her shy away?"

Belle sipped her drink and thought it over. "I reckon you wouldn't," she concluded. "It's a deal."

"Tell Gil not to waste any time. If it's not done before the tenth of July the deal's off."

Canby booked a room at the Idaho City hotel. In the morning he could make a show of inspecting the old Bascomb property and then ride back to Boise City.

From his room window he watched the street and presently he saw a livery boy tie a buggy in front of Belle Plover's saloon. No doubt she'd used it before, perhaps to deliver liquor at some placer camp or to buy moonshine at a hideaway still. The woman came out with a half-filled flour sack and in the fading twilight drove north toward the timbered hills dividing this basin from the Payette watershed. The sack might hold food or a warm coat for Gil Henry at some woods cabin.

The odds, Canby calculated, were now doubled against Marcus Lindsay and Verne Hallam. Gil Henry was sure to go after them. And so, quite likely, would the remnants of the Floyd Plover gang, who had both a revenge and a security motive. Gresham and Hallam were potential

155

court witnesses against them. There was a fair chance they'd beat Gil to the kill.

Gil, though, would have an advantage. The five now aflight from Massacre Canyon would have posses beating the bush for them. They might have neither time nor stomach for another raid on the Stanley camp.

With Gil Henry it was different. His trail from Montana was cold now. With no local law barking at his heels he could pick a dark night and creep up on the three sleeping campers. Warren Stanley he needn't touch. Only Lindsay and Hallam.

CHAPTER XIII

"We'll let 'em graze here a couple of days, John," Warren Stanley said to his teamster, "till we hear from Paul."

A pair of Bliss Ranch riders had helped them swim the cows to the north bank of the Snake River and Marcus Lindsay had made a comfortable camp here. "What then?" he asked as he kindled the supper fire.

"I told Paul to hire a drover and send him down. Soon as the man gets here we'll push on up the trail. Only ninety-odd miles more of it."

Lindsay looked across the Snake to the settlement of Glenn's Ferry where they'd buried Floyd Plover. The ferry itself was drawn up at a ramp on this side of the river, waiting for today's stage from Boise City, which was soon due.

Side meat was sizzling in a pan when the stage came in sight. It rattled past them and bore down on the ferry. "Maybe I can pick up a newspaper, John."

Warren walked a hundred yards to the ferry ramp and Lindsay saw him speak to the stage driver. Something the driver said seemed to excite Warren. Lindsay saw him follow the coach across the gang-bridge and continue asking questions on the ferry's deck. Passengers got out of the coach to help the driver answer them. The ferryman himself joined the group and delayed passage for a few minutes.

Then Warren jumped ashore and hurried to join Lindsay at camp. He didn't bring a Boise City paper. "But I've got news just the same."

"About Paul?"

"Paul sent word everything's fine. He's mending fast. Remember what we heard about a cowboy named Hallam? The one who chased robbers away from Nan's stagecoach? He's coming down to help on the drive."

"He'll come by saddle?"

"No. By buckboard with his riding horse tied behind. He'll come back with the Bliss hand who took Paul to Boise City."

"What about that kid deputy who went up with them?"

A grimness came to Warren's face. "You mean Chuck Prather. Bad news about him. He's dead. Ambushed on his way to Silver City in a gorge they call Massacre Canyon. Him and the stage driver and a salesman who happened to be on the same stage. They figure it was pals of Floyd Plover because it was done to rescue Prather's prisoners. Posses from two counties are trying to track 'em."

"How many?"

"Three waylaid the coach. Makes five of 'em on the loose, counting the two they took off the stage. The same pair of scamps you tied into with a shotgun, John. Last seen, the five were heading toward lower Bruneau Creek."

"Which is where?"

Warren pointed down the Snake River. "Bruneau Creek comes in about twenty miles below here, from the other side."

"Find out anything else?"

"Yes. Good news along with the bad. Paul had Nan and the cowboy Hallam check on that ranch ad. The place looks good and Paul's gonna sign a lease. We can take the cows straight to it."

"Then we won't have to go through town?"

"Not with the cows and the wagon. Town's on the other side of the Boise River and the ranch is on this side. That stew smells good, John. Dish me up a pan of it."

When darkness came Marcus Lindsay lay long awake, alternately relieved and fearful. It was a welcome relief to know he wouldn't have to drive his wagon up Main Street with sidewalk crowds staring at him. They'd naturally be curious to see the man who, in a midnight gunfight with all the odds against him, had killed Floyd Plover and captured two of his gang. The reaction in Boise City, according to passing travelers, had been sensational. "Everybody in town," a trailsman had told Lindsay, "will want to buy you a drink."

For Lindsay a spotlight like that was a thing to be dreaded. He wanted to be unimportant and unnoticed. First he must see Lois and the boy without letting them see him. Second he must find out if a man named Canby was on the level.

The latter mission seemed all but hopeless. Half a dozen times since hearing camp gossip from Earnshaw on Raft Creek he'd been tempted to quit the Stanleys and slip quietly away. Nothing was to be gained by staying on here and everything was to be lost—everything, that is, except a thin possibility of saving Lois from a tragic mistake. It would be a mistake only if Canby long ago had headed a ring of bogus dust passers.

Yet again tonight Marcus Lindsay came stubbornly back to his Raft Creek decision. Even if there was only one chance in a thousand that Canby was a scamp, he must still make sure of it before moving on. Just how he had no idea. And he had less than three weeks to work in—three short weeks before the deadline of a wedding date. July the tenth, according to the papers.

Another June day came and passed lazily, with three hundred young cows resting and feeding on riverbank grass. Shortly before sundown a buckboard hove in sight. Two cowboys were in it and the youngest of them had three shades of red between his hatbrim and his doeskin jacket. A riding horse came trotting along behind. "Here we are," Gunther announced as he reined up at the Stanley wagon. "Boys, meet Verne Hallam from Kansas."

Warren shook hands heartily. "Reckon Paul's already thanked you for getting Nan out of a jamb. This is our wagon man, John Gresham."

As Hallam looked at him, Lindsay couldn't miss the quick and inevitable reaction mirrored in his face and eyes. He'd been seeing it for ten years. Usually it was a mixture of pity and revulsion. With women it was always more noticeable than with men. "How frightful!" the look said.

On Verne Hallam's ruddy young face it was only fleeting. "You've got the whole town talkin' about you, Gresham," he said. "I'll be mighty proud to ride with you."

The shy disquiet which came over the teamster went unnoticed. Verne took his saddle gear and bedroll from the buckboard and put his roan horse on picket. Gunther, after stopping only for a cup of coffee, drove on to catch the next ferry.

After supper Warren Stanley asked: "What about those five men on the run from killing Chuck Prather?"

"Last I heard they're still on the loose," Verne said. He turned grimly toward Lindsay. "They're old friends of yours and mine, pardner. The way Robbins figures it, three of 'em were with Floyd Plover when they sneaked up on you the other night. The other two beat the hell out of me in an empty house."

"Let's hope they don't come this way," Warren said.

"They might, at that," Verne countered. "Folks say they're just mean enough to try to get even with Gresham. They say if we're wise we'll post a guard every night till those five buggers are locked up."

"We'll do that," Warren decided. "Each of us can stand a three-hour trick. Pick any watch you want, men, and I'll take what's left."

Lindsay was given the first trick, nine till midnight. He kept the fire burning but stayed out of its glow, sitting with his back to a cottonwood and with a shotgun across his knees. He liked the cut of young Hallam. Maybe the cowboy could help dig up the truth about Canby. According to letters from Nan, both Hallam and the girl had been dinner guests of Lois Lindsay with Canby present. He wondered what the cowboy thought of Canby. *Soon as I get to know him better, I'll ask him.*

At midnight Warren relieved Lindsay. "Better get hitched by sunup, John. We want to make fifteen miles tomorrow."

The fifteen miles were made handily and it put them half way from Glenn's Ferry to the relay station of Rattlesnake. Today for security, Warren made Lindsay follow instead of lead with the wagon. "Can't let you get too far away from us, John, with those killers on the loose."

In the evening Lindsay had no more than unhitched when he saw a lone rider approaching at right angles from the south. As the man came up his brass badge identified him as a lawman. "It's Bud Akins," Verne Hallam said. "I met him at Marshal Robbins's office. He's one of the deputies who took off after those killers."

"Looks kinda young to be out manhunting," Warren remarked. And indeed Bud Akins, as he dismounted, seemed barely out of his teens, perhaps a year or two younger than Chuck Prather, who'd been killed in Reynolds Creek Canyon.

"Is this the Stanley outfit?" Akins asked. "Robbins told me to string along with you for the next few days. Just to play safe. What about a cup of coffee?" He had a jaded look and his eyes were bloodshot from hard riding in the wind.

Lindsay soon had supper on. Two posses, Bud Akins explained, were looking for outlaw sign south of the Snake. "We followed it to Jack's Creek and then lost it. Robbins's crew is trying to pick it up on the Bruneau and the Owyhee County posse is workin' the Wickahoney. Chances are ten to one those killers are heading up one of those creeks toward Nevada."

"Then what are you doing here in the opposite direction?" Hallam queried.

"Because the one-to-ten chance is that they crossed the Snake and are making for the high country north of here." Akins thumbed toward the lofty peaks of the Sawtooth Range. "If they do they'd cross the Overland Trail about here and I understand they've got it in for your teamster." Bud looked at Lindsay with a boyish grin. "Can't blame 'em, the way he made 'em look bad that time."

So Orlando Robbins had dispatched one of his men to join the Stanley drive. "It'll give you an extra gun in case Frank Hugo and his devils pay a get-even call on you boys."

"Frank Hugo?"

Akins nodded. "Robbins figures he's taken over now that Floyd Plover's gone. He's the long skinny guy who got away the night Lindsay downed Plover."

Bud Akins's presence shortened the night watches to two hours each for the four men. "We can make Rattlesnake by sundown," Akins said at breakfast.

He added his saddle horse to the two remounts tied to the endgate of Lindsay's wagon and got in under canvas with a repeating rifle by him. Lindsay, sitting alone on the driver's seat, clucked to his mules. "Let's go, Tom. Move along, Jerry." The wagon moved off and again, as on every day except yesterday, Lindsay drove well ahead of the cattle.

Lindsay himself had suggested it and after some hesitation Warren Stanley had agreed. "It's kinda like using you for bait, Gresham," Bud Akins said. "But there's no risk with me out of sight in the wagon."

The theory was that if Hugo's gang were heading for the Sawtooths they'd need to travel by night and lie low by day. If they were holed up under cover all day they could be watching this trail for posse men. Marcus Lindsay, apparently alone and driving his wagon a mile or so ahead of his outfit, would look like an easy mark and might tempt an attack. Before they learned better, Bud's repeating rifle would be spouting bullets at them. "Not to mention your shotgun," Bud said.

It was a thin chance at best and today the chance became even thinner because of extra traffic on the trail. In midmorning they caught up with a wagon train of landseekers heading for Oregon. The wagons were moving only a little slower than Lindsay's and he couldn't conveniently pass them. "No chance of Hugo comin' at us today," Bud Akins said. "Too many witnesses."

When at sundown they got to Rattlesnake the stage from Boise City was changing horses there. It was a swing station and the incoming driver was at the end of his run. He spied Lindsay's wagon and came up with a wide grin. "I bet you're John Gresham. My name's Harbison. It

165

was my coach that Nan Stanley was on when she got held up. Where's Hallam?"

An answer came from Bud Akins who appeared from under the wagon's canvas. "He's not far behind us, Dan, helping Warren Stanley bring along the cows."

Dan Harbison produced a letter addressed to Warren. "His sister asked me to fetch it along and leave it with the stationmaster in case I missed you. That gal's havin' a right busy time."

"You mean fixing up the ranch house?" Lindsay asked.

Harbison nodded. "Window curtains, rugs, cushions and a brand-new parlor set. She's out there every day with a strong-armed Irishwoman scrubbing floors and windows. Some of the town ladies are helpin'. Specially Lois Lindsay. She's sort of taking Nan under her wing. Soon as you make camp, Gresham, come over to the station bar and I'll buy you a drink."

But Lindsay, after making camp half a mile up a water run, kept resolutely away from the station bar. He didn't want people making a fuss over him. A nervous fear grew inside of him. He'd hoped to avoid stares by driving his wagon straight to the fenced section eight miles from town, where only the Stanleys would see him. Now he sensed that others would be there for some sort of a house warming or welcoming party! What if Lois herself should

166

be here! How could he hide his face from her?

His fears were compounded when Warren buoy-antly read Nan's letter aloud to his campmates. "Listen to this, fellas:"

> You can't imagine how wonderful every-one is to us, Warren. Both our country neighbors and people from town. Today they made a regular picnic of it, fried chicken and all, everyone helping me fix up the house. Tomorrow I'll buy furniture at Mr. Falk's store and Mr. Agnew is lending a wagon to haul it out there. The doctor says Paul can move out day after tomorrow. We can hardly wait to see you drive those cows through the gate. And guess what! I'll have a grand supper party that evening. There'll be you and Paul and me and Verne Hallam and that blessed Mr. Gresham who saved you from the outlaws. And of course Mrs. Lindsay and her boy Mark, and her fiancé Mr. Canby. You can't imagine how sweet and kind Mrs. Lindsay has been to me.

There was more of it—and as Marcus Lindsay listened a sweat of panic broke out over him. The Stanley section was only fifty miles away and he'd be there in four more days. He wanted to see Lois but not face to face across a supper table. He couldn't meet a test like that. Already he could feel her eyes on him, searching him through the scars and pits of his skin.

The man who called himself John Gresham withdrew from the others, his mind flinching from the crisis now only four days and four nights away. He had just that long in which to conjure up some way to avoid the home-coming welcome. Could he desert his wagon and run just before reaching the ranch gate? Could he hide in a barn loft? How could he see, and not at short range be seen by, a woman he loved and a son he didn't even know?

CHAPTER XIV

An impatient eagerness made Warren and Verne push the cattle a full sixteen miles the next day. It seemed to Lindsay that Verne was no less eager than Warren, as though he too were approaching a family and home. A certain dreamy look on the cowboy's face while Warren was reading Nan's letter gave a hint of the answer. Verne Hallam had spent several adventurous days with Nan Stanley and it wouldn't be strange if he was already in love with her. Unconsciously Verne was using the word "we" when talking about the Stanley affairs. The *Tri-Weekly Statesman*, in its first news story about the Kansas cowboy, had said he'd soon move on to Oregon. Now he said nothing about Oregon.

They camped near a relay station with the strange name of Soul's Rest. And again there was a letter from Nan. Again Warren read it aloud to his campmates. Verne's face, as he listened, had the same glow. "Looks like we've got some right good neighbors," he said to Warren.

During the day's drive they'd crossed a stream called Canyon Creek and Lindsay, fording it with his wagon, had noticed trout darting through its clear pools. A fisherman in hip boots had waved at him.

The man's face seemed dimly familiar and Lindsay was sure he must have known him in the old days around Boise or Idaho City. He couldn't place the name and it was clear that the fisherman didn't recognize Lindsay.

Encounters like that always served to bolster Lindsay's confidence. After making camp that evening he joined Warren, Verne and Bud Akins as they walked over to the Soul's Rest station to ask for mail. The Canyon Creek fisherman was eating supper there. He was spending the night here and planned to go back to Boise City on tomorrow's stage.

Bud Akins knew him quite well. "Howdy, Mr. Moore. Meet Warren Stanley, who figures to settle on the Ab Brown place. This here's his trail crew, Verne Hallam and John Gresham."

"I met your brother Paul," the fisherman said warmly to Warren. "I banked a five thousand dollar draft for him. Saw you in town too, Hallam." His heartiest greeting was for Marcus Lindsay. "You're the toast of the town, Gresham, on account of that shotgun job you did on the Plover gang. Drop in at the bank some day and I'll take you to the Idaho Club for lunch."

Now Lindsay placed him.

He was C. W. Moore, who ten years ago had been cashier of the Boise City bank, with a finger in every big mining deal in two counties.

"A letter for you, Mr. Stanley," the station man said. "And for you too, Mr. Gresham."

The one for John Gresham was a short, graceful note.

> Dear Mr. Gresham:
>
> My brothers are very precious to me and except for you I would have lost them both. Please know that a welcome awaits you at our new home and we want you to share it with us, just like one of the family.
>
> Gratefully yours,
> Nan Stanley.

Lindsay folded the note carefully and put it in his wallet. Would she still feel that way, he wondered, after she saw his face?

Banker Moore, at least, hadn't recognized him and neither had Milton Kelly. But they'd only known him distantly. They'd have no reason to remember an unimportant miner of the Sixties. With Lois it would be different. She'd know his voice even if she didn't at once know his face.

Again Lindsay spent a troubled night on the horns of a dilemma trying to conjure up a way to avoid an encounter with Lois. Short of an abrupt desertion of his job he could think of no way at all. In the morning his eyes showed that he hadn't slept.

"You feeling under the weather, John?" Warren asked.

Lindsay murmured an evasion and went to harness the mules. Verne was already asaddle to bunch the cattle.

"I've been thinking," Bud Akins said. "We've only got one more trail camp. Dunn's station. Between here and there we cross Indian Creek. Which is where Verne had his run-in with the Plover gang."

Warren looked at his trail map. "That's right. So what?"

"If the Plover gang wants to get even," Akins suggested, "they might pick that same spot to do it. They could use the same cover Verne used. And while they're at it they could knock over both Gresham and Hallam. It'd wipe the slate clean and give 'em a good laugh on the side."

Verne rode up and they talked it over. "Forewarned is forearmed," Warren decided. "So today we'll let the wagon follow the cows close up. Bud, you ride under canvas with your rifle primed."

The drive started and today they kept on the stage road. The cows strung out along it, at times impeding the progress of immigrant wagons heading west.

In midmorning the stage from Kelton overtook and passed them. It would make a meal stop at Dunn's and be in Boise City by four in the afternoon.

Soon after that the cattle drive came to the spot where the coach bearing Nan Stanley and Lois Lindsay had been held up three weeks ago. A hawk circled lazily over the brushy hillock from which Hallam had fired on Floyd Plover. This time there was no shooting. The drive moved on and crossed Indian Creek, the heifers lowing rebelliously when the drovers prodded them, snatching at bits of trailside grass whenever they got a chance.

"False alarm," Bud said with a sheepish grin.

"We're not out of the woods yet," Warren warned. Any roadside ditch or thicket could still make cover for snipers.

The drive moved sluggishly on and it was past sundown when they sighted Dunn's relay station. "They serve right good grub," Verne remembered. "We ate there right after the hold-up. Your sister and Mrs. Lindsay and I—and Dan Harbison, and a guy named Rogan."

"Tell you what," Warren decided. "This'll be our last night stop, so let's celebrate. You won't need to fix a camp supper, John. We'll just bunch the stuff at stock water and picket the remounts. Then we'll all eat at the relay station. On me."

Convenient stock water was a half mile short of the station and a half mile north of the trail. When the cows had watered there and began foraging, the four men rode to the stage station and dismounted.

A man with a broad swarthy face came out to meet them and drew a stare of surprise from Bud Akins. "What the dickens are you doing here, Pedro? Has Robbins called off the manhunt?"

"No," Pedro said. "But he sends me with a message for you. If you will come to the bar I will explain."

As the two deputies headed for the station's bar, Warren Stanley went to the dining room and ordered a steak supper for his crew. Presently Bud Akins and Pedro rejoined them.

"Marshal Robbins knows for sure now," Bud explained, "that the five killers didn't ride this way on a get-even spree. They went in the opposite direction, south toward Nevada. Robbins found out they raided a ranch on the upper Bruneau for grub and fresh horses. Last seen they were ninety miles from here and riding south."

So Orlando Robbins had sent Pedro to intercept and recall Bud Akins. In the morning the two deputies would ride to rejoin the posse. "Which means I've been wastin' my time," Bud said.

"You've been good company," Warren told him. "Pull up a chair, Pedro. It's my treat. What about a bottle of wine, Mr. Dunn?"

"Anyways," Bud grinned, "we can all get a good night's sleep. No use postin' watches, with Hugo and company ninety miles from here."

All but Lindsay were in a mood to celebrate.

174

For Marcus Lindsay the steak and wine dinner was wasted. He had no taste for it and at the first opportunity excused himself. "If you don't mind, boys, I'll go turn in."

He left them and went out to his horse. It was a mile to the wagon and almost dark when he got there. A scattering of dim stars appeared. Lindsay made a fire to light and warm the others when they came to camp.

After unsaddling his horse he led it some fifty yards to where the remounts were picketed. The mules were loose and grazing nearby. Scrubby timber grew on a gentle upslope from the camp and Lindsay heard a dry branch crackle. Maybe one of the cows was bedding down up there.

Back at the wagon he took his blanket roll and as usual carried it well apart from the fire, spreading it on level sand. Then a voice spoke from the gloom and it was one he'd never heard before. "Do like I say, Gresham."

A gun was pressing against the small of his back and a hand slapped his pockets to see if he was armed. He wasn't. The shotgun was on the wagon seat where it had been all day. Marcus Lindsay had never in his life carried a revolver.

Raising his arms slowly he turned for a look at the man back of him. The dim night light revealed a man of medium height, shabbily dressed, stockily built and bearded. "Did Hugo send you?"

"Who's Hugo?" The man's tone and vacant stare somehow led Lindsay to conclude the gunman had no connection with Hugo.

"Turn around and cross your hands behind your back."

When Lindsay obeyed, loops were noosed over his wrists and the cords drawn tightly. "Let's go, Gresham."

With his hands tied behind him and a gun punching his back, Lindsay was marched north up the hillside. After a stumbling walk of perhaps ten minutes he found himself in a thicket where two saddled horses were tied. "This one's yours, Gresham. Put your foot in a stirrup and I'll boost you up."

The click as the man cocked his gun convinced Lindsay that he'd be shot dead on the spot if he didn't do as ordered. When his left foot was in a stirrup a boost from the gunman put him astride a saddle. One by one his ankles were tied to the stirrups. The horse had no bridle, only a lead rope. The gunman got on the other horse and rode upslope, leading Lindsay's.

"I've got friends who can follow tracks."

"Not in the dark," the man ahead said. "We've got all night to lose our sign. Just sit tight and keep your mouth shut."

They topped a hill and in a valley beyond it splashed into water, riding a long way up that water with overhanging willows slapping them.

Three times during the night they rode water. One of the streams was deep and wide, its current wetting Lindsay to the knees. It was certain to be the Boise River. No other stream that big lay in this direction.

Beyond the river they rode for miles up a canyon and then turned up a steep mountainside. After a long climb Lindsay saw the shapes of trees and by the smell knew they were pines. From a trail map he knew that a pine-topped mountain lay just northeast of Boise City. Shaw's Mountain, the map said.

They circled the lip of that mountain, high up, and when day began breaking came to an abandoned mine tunnel. The gunman rode into it and dismounted. He helped Lindsay from his saddle. "Here's where we hole up for the day, Gresham."

He tied the prisoner's ankles together but untied the hands. Then he produced a sack of hardtack and a canteen. Lindsay sat with his back against the tunnel's wall. "What have you got against me?" he asked.

"Not a thing, Gresham. All I want's to make sure I get paid."

"Paid what?"

"Ten thousand dollars. You're in somebody's way, Mister."

"If he offered you ten thousand dollars to kill me, why don't you?"

"I will—soon as I collect. Only way I can keep him from welshing."

Lindsay began to understand. "I see. After you shoot me I'll be out of his way. And when I'm out of his way he'll have no reason to pay."

"That's it. And nothing to pay with either. I've just found out he's broke. Puts on a big front but the only way he could raise ten thousand'd be to steal it or borrow it from a bank. Which he won't bother to do unless I put the squeeze on him."

"The squeeze being the fact that I'm still alive?"

The gunman rolled a cigaret. "You catch on quick, Mister. Long as you're alive I can make him say Papa. But I'll need somethin' to show him. So I can prove I've got you. Somethin' personal like nobody but you could have."

He came over and searched Lindsay's pockets. There was a small knife, a few coins, a handkerchief and a thin wallet. The man helped himself to the wallet's money but was mainly interested in a folded paper. It was a note in a girl's handwriting.

"This'll do." The man pouched Nan Stanley's thank-you letter and moved back across the tunnel. He squatted there, chewing hardtack, then tossed a piece of it to his prisoner.

"Who are you?" Lindsay hardly expected an answer but got one.

"You can call me Gil."

"Where are you taking me?"

"A far piece. We'll need to travel two more nights."

"This man who wants me out of the way. Who is he?"

"Never mind. He just wants you dead, that's all. If you was to turn up alive you'd make a mess for him. When I prove I've got you alive I'll have him where the hair's short. If he tries to welsh I could . . ."

"You could do what?"

A crafty gleam came to the man's eyes. "I could turn you loose on a lady's front lawn, alive and kicking, on the tenth of July."

"Why the tenth of July?"

"It's a deadline, Gresham. By then you're dead if he pays—and he's cooked if he don't."

"It's the day he's getting married," Lindsay said. "And his name's Canby."

A feeling strangely like relief came over him. Yesterday's dilemma no longer preyed upon him and was now taken completely out of his hands. Over it he no longer had the power of decision. Fate had made the decision for him.

And tonight, at a homecoming supper party, he wouldn't need to face Lois Lindsay.

CHAPTER XV

Driving Lois out to a party at the Stanley ranch was the last thing Wade Canby wanted to do. But there was no way to avoid it. Without consulting him, Lois had gaily accepted Nan's invitation. "I wouldn't miss it for anything, Wade. We must be sure to get there before the trail herd does. Is the Overland stage in yet, do you suppose?"

"Not yet."

The coach from Kelton was due at four o'clock. It was a little past four now. Canby, having picked Lois up at her house, trotted his livery rig down Seventh Street to the Boise River ferry. It would be midnight before they got home and Lois, not wanting Mark to stay up that late, had left the boy with Helga.

They were ferried to the south bank and Lois decided to wait there for the overdue stage. It should be along in a few minutes and the driver could tell them just where he'd passed the trail herd. "Then we can tell Nan. Nothing is more important to a hostess than to know in advance just when her guests will arrive."

"Maybe," Canby said with a shrug, "they won't get here before tomorrow."

"Maybe," Lois admitted. "But we know that yesterday's stage passed them near Indian Creek which would put them at Dunn's by sundown. With an early start from Dunn's they can get all the way home before dark tonight."

"If they force the pace," Canby agreed.

"And why shouldn't they? Warren Stanley will be impatient to see his new ranch. And Verne Hallam will be just as eager to see Nan."

"Here it comes," Canby said.

A stage coach hove in sight and rattled down the hill to the ferry's ramp. Dan Harbison held the reins. "Where did you pass them, Dan?" Lois asked him. "The Stanley trail herd?"

"Just a little piece back." There was an odd note of gravity in the driver's answer. "They're coming fast and ought to be at the ranch gate by dark. But Warren's not with 'em. Neither is the wagon man Gresham. Seems like they had some bad luck in camp near Dunn's station."

"Bad luck? You mean there was an accident?"

"They ain't sure what happened," Dan Harbison said. "The mule skinner, Gresham, disappeared last night. Maybe he just walked off. Or maybe he was hepped off at the point of a gun. No sign of any shooting. Nothing was stolen. The rest of the crew did some celebrating at the station last night. When they got back to camp Gresham just wasn't there."

Canby's pulse quickened. He couldn't doubt

but that Gil Henry had earned his murder fee last night. He must have marched his man away beyond earshot before pulling the trigger. In due time they'd find the body in some gully or brush pile.

"I can hardly believe it!" Lois Lindsay exclaimed in dismay.

"Warren Stanley and a couple of deputies are looking for him," Dan told her. "Two of Dunn's corral men offered to help Verne Hallam push the herd this way. Verne'll tell you all about it. They asked me to report it to Oldham's office. Giddap!" He drove his coach across the ramp to the ferry's deck.

Lois looked dismally at her escort. "Now we're bearers of *bad* news instead of good!"

Bad news for everyone but me! Canby thought with subdued elation.

He'd been on tenterhooks of dread ever since learning that Lindsay was alive and on his way to Boise City. It was a cumulative dread which would have funneled to a nerve-smashing climax at the Stanley supper table tonight, with Marcus and Lois Lindsay facing each other. Would the man announce himself? Would the woman recognize the man? In either case Wade Canby's own prospects would be blighted.

Now, thanks to Gil Henry, he could breathe freely again.

What about Gil's fee? The ten thousand dollars?

Let him whistle for it, Canby decided as he drove Lois on down the river trail.

"Do you suppose," she asked fearfully, "that one of those Plover outlaws did it?"

"Who else? They had it in for him. He shotgunned them one time, killed their leader and made them look bad. I hear five of them are being chased by posses. But they've got friends in Boise City. Dunn's is only sixteen miles down the road. It's the closest trail camp where they could get at him."

Lois shuddered. "Do you really think so?"

"Who else," Canby repeated, "would do it?"

Lawmen and laymen at the county seat would say the same thing. Only the Plover gang and their allies of the Boise City underworld would have it in for the wagoneer. On that same ground of logic Canby himself, when Belle Henry came around for her money, could refuse payment. "Look, Belle. Why should I pay Gil when he didn't do it?"

In any case Canby had no choice. He couldn't possibly raise ten thousand dollars. Only today he'd sounded out the bank and been turned down. Raising a few hundred dollars for a wedding trip would be difficult enough. After that his financial problems should smooth out. A wealthy wife would expect him to manage her affairs and Wade Canby knew just how to do it.

● ● ●

In the dimming twilight Nan and Paul Stanley stood solemnly on the house porch and watched three hundred tired heifers straggle through the pasture gate. Behind them came Verne Hallam and a corral man from Dunn's named Brady. Another of Dunn's men, Job Walsh, was driving the trail wagon. It was to have been a joyful homecoming. But now, because a wagoneer was missing and possibly dead, all the cheer was gone from it.

Wade Canby stood at the other end of the porch, puffing a cigar. Lois was inside helping the brawny Irishwoman put supper on. "You watch for Verne Hallam," she'd said to Nan.

Nan saw Verne close the pasture gate and ride on to the barn. After corralling his roan he came dejectedly to the house.

"You've heard?" he asked Nan.

"Yes. The stage driver told Mrs. Lindsay."

"I feel it's my fault," Verne muttered. "I should've kept an eye on him."

Canby strolled down the porch and joined them. "Don't blame yourself, Hallam. Those Plover devils were sure to get him, sooner or later. Have they found his body?"

"They hadn't when I left," Verne said. "And maybe they won't. Maybe he just walked out on us."

"Walked out on you?" Canby's tone seemed startled. "Why would he do that?"

184

"Yes. Why?" Nan echoed.

"I don't know," Verne brooded. "But somehow I got the idea that Gresham was leery about coming into Boise City. Every time we talked about it he drew back into a shell. The nearer we got to town the worse it was. You sent him a thank-you note, Nan. I saw him read it and there was a sort of a scared look on his face. Pretty soon he went back to camp by himself. That was at Soul's Rest. A night later we found his bedroll empty and cold."

When the two men from Dunn's came up Nan took them all in to supper. But what had been planned as a gay party was spoiled now.

There was a single thread of hope and Nan clung to it. "Verne thinks that maybe Mr. Gresham was just timid about joining us, Lois, and so maybe he slipped away on purpose."

"It's barely possible," Verne said.

"I got the same idea myself," Paul Stanley said, "as far back as the Raft Creek camp. Shy about meeting people, I guess. Maybe it's because folks have stared at that burned face of his till he wants to stay off by himself."

The corral man Brady had a thought. "Might be he was in trouble one time at Boise City. A long time ago. Say he busted outa jail and is leery about showin' up here again. He can't admit it to his boss. So at the last trail camp before gettin' here he ducks out."

"He's no jailbird," Paul argued stoutly.

"We might as well face it," Wade Canby put in. "Five of the Plover outlaws are a long way off and just a jump ahead of a posse. But some ally of theirs in town could easily have slipped down to Dunn's last night."

"Lew Rogan, for instance?" Verne asked quietly.

His steady stare brought a flush to Canby. "Rogan? Why Rogan?"

"Because just before he was shot, Plover mentioned Rogan. 'Either you're a liar,' he said, 'or Lew is.'"

Nan, looking at Canby's taut face, had a feeling he was braced to resist a challenge. Lois and Paul missed it. Only to Nan had Verne intimated a distrust of Canby. After an uneasy silence the man's answer came with a studied caution.

"Lots of Lews in Idaho. What makes you think Plover meant Lew Rogan?"

"Because Rogan's a pussy-footer." Verne's eyes still held Canby's. "He had a pussy-footing visitor at one o'clock in the morning the night of the post dance—somebody who sneaked out a window when I knocked on the door."

"But Verne!" Nan exclaimed in surprise. "Why didn't you tell me?"

"Haven't seen you since then. Early the next morning I left for Glenn's Ferry."

Lois Lindsay looked confused. "Do you mean," she asked, "that you went to Rogan's room after midnight and found somebody already there?"

Verne nodded. "Someone who slipped out a window to keep me from catching him."

"Who could it have been?" Nan wondered.

"I didn't see him and they were talking in whispers," Verne said. "It was right after Chuck Prather had reported Plover's last words. Somebody who went hot-foot to warn Lew Rogan."

More than that Verne Hallam couldn't say. Canby was Nan's guest and Lois Lindsay's fiancé. All he could do was put pressure on the man and hope he'd crack.

"You think it was Rogan," Paul prompted bluntly, "who got to Gresham last night?"

"Either Rogan or the man I almost caught in his room," Verne said. "Tomorrow I'll find out where Rogan was at ten o'clock last night."

"You won't need to wait till tomorrow," Wade Canby said smoothly. "I can tell you right now." His voice was again calm and confident. "At ten last night I happened to meet John Hailey in front of the Bonanza. We went in for a nightcap and saw Lew Rogan in a card game. You can check it with Hailey if you like."

Nan saw a look of bafflement on Verne's face. No-one could doubt an alibi supported by John

Hailey. "So Rogan couldn't have gone to Dunn's last night!"

"No, he couldn't," Verne admitted. In blank frustration his mind added: *Nor could his pussyfooting visitor, Wade Canby.*

CHAPTER XVI

After an early breakfast Verne rode upriver with the two corralmen from Dunn's. They'd stayed overnight in the upper rooms as guests of the Stanleys. Lois Lindsay and Wade Canby had driven back to town soon after supper.

"Jimmie Dunn told us to hurry home," Brady said. "He needs us to relay stage teams."

"Thanks a lot," Verne said, "for helping me bring on the cows."

At the ferry they left him and rode down the Overland Trail toward Dunn's. Verne wanted to go with them and help Warren in his search for Gresham. But Bud Akins and Pedro were already helping Warren and perhaps by now Sheriff Oldham had sent some county deputies there.

"I'll likely do more good in town," Verne said to the ferryman as he crossed to the town side of the river.

"It sure was a rum deal," the ferryman said, "that wagon driver gettin' gunned in the dark. Feelings are runnin' plenty high, from what I hear. If they ketch whoever done it there could easy be a neck-stretchin' party."

Verne rode on to Agnew's barn and put up his horse. In the barn's corral he saw the pack mare he'd brought from Kansas. "Paul Stanley," the

189

corral man said, "offers to pasture her free at his new ranch, Mr. Hallam. Shall I send her out?"

"I'll let you know," Verne said.

He hurried to the Overland Stage office and called on John Hailey. "Good morning, Mr. Hailey. I understand you and Wade Canby happened to see Lew Rogan in a card game at ten o'clock night before last. It was at the Bonanza on Idaho Street."

"We did. You're looking for the man who killed or kidnapped Gresham at a trail camp near Dunn's, I take it?"

"That's right, I am. So it wasn't Rogan. Thanks, Mr. Hailey."

Verne registered at the Overland and was given the same room he'd had before. He put his saddle roll in it. From there he walked a block to the sheriff's office.

Only a jailor and Deputy Ben Alanson were there. "Sheriff Oldham took a couple of the boys and went down to Dunn's last night," Alanson reported.

He struck Verne as an officer of more than average intelligence and he decided to confide his suspicions. For the first time he told about Lew Rogan's furtive slipping of the message into Wade Canby's pocket, following this with a statement about the after-midnight call at Rogan's room. "Whoever was in there with him sneaked out a window and down a balcony to another room. I'll lay odds it was Canby."

The deputy listened, then shook his head with a tongue-in-cheek smile. "You may be right about Rogan but you're dead wrong about Canby. Canby's a top level citizen. Ask anybody and they'll tell you the same: Milt Kelly, John Hailey, C. W. Moore. Or Lois Lindsay. She's the cream of Idaho society and she wouldn't marry herself off to a no-gooder. Rogan might fill your hand, Hallam, but you'd better discard Canby."

"Then why did Rogan slip the note in his pocket?"

Alanson shrugged. "It's quite likely that Canby uses Rogan as an errand-runner now and then. No harm in that. Maybe Rogan wanted to report on some small errand, like passing on an address or a price he'd dug up. Canby had just helped his lady out of a stagecoach and there was a crowd around them. Oldham and Robbins were getting a report about the Indian Creek hold-up. You were in the crowd and so was the Stanley girl. Rather than barge in on a talk-fest like that, Rogan simply dropped a slip of paper into Canby's pocket. Nothing on it except a name or an address or maybe a price."

Verne was only partially impressed. "Very well. Then what about the one A.M. visitor who slipped out Rogan's window?"

The deputy grinned wisely. "I can see you haven't had much experience, young fella. Ten-to-one the visitor was a woman and when you knocked she thought it was her husband. So she flits."

Again Verne was less than half convinced. "Any word from the Owyhee County posses?"

"Only that they're chasing five men and we've got the leader tabbed as Frank Hugo. He's a long lanky guy who escaped from the trail camp raid where Gresham killed Plover. He ought to have a bullet scar on his arm where you pinked him down at Indian Creek. Two others are Schulte and a guy named Joad, alias Bob Baker. That's the pair Chuck Prather was taking to the Silver City jail."

"The other two," Verne concluded, "are the ones who helped Hugo rescue Schulte and Joad."

Alanson nodded grimly. "Rescued 'em by killing everybody else on the stage. We think their names are Webber and Shoop. Shoop's the guy with the round, red-stubbled face that you and Robbins ran into when someone shot out the lights at Dutch Henry's bar."

Verne thought it over. "Which leaves," he summed up, "at least one member of the gang still on the loose here in town."

"At least one," Alanson agreed. "The guy who shot out the lights."

"Got any idea who he is?"

The deputy nodded shrewdly. "We can't prove it, but we've a hunch he's Luke France. Luke was there—and he's a trick shot with a six-gun. Put on an exhibition one time at the county fair. Last summer he was tried for a killing but two alibi witnesses got him off. Later one of those witnesses was shot dead while helping the Plover gang hold up the Silver City bank."

"How do you know he was at Dutch Henry's that night?" In the darkness everyone but Verne himself, Robbins, Paxton and Dutch Henry had scampered out of the barroom.

"We found a storekeeper on Fifth Street," Alanson explained, "who saw 'em pilin' out the front door. The first man out was a guy with a long, narrow face, handlebar mustaches and a belted gun. He had on brown corduroys and a flat Texas hat turned up in front. Meets the description of Luke France. We've been looking for France but can't locate him. If you run onto him, ask him where he was at ten o'clock night before last."

"You think maybe he killed Gresham at the camp near Dunn's?"

"He's the likeliest suspect we've got. And if you think a minute you'll see why."

"Because shooting out the lights ties him to the Plover gang. And only the Plover gang were out to get Gresham."

"That's only part of it. Remember what Plover said to Warren Stanley? 'Either you're a liar or Lew is.' "

Verne didn't at once see the connection. "So what?"

"Maybe what he really said was: 'Either you're a liar or *Luke* is.'"

When it sank in Verne was impressed. The man who'd shot out the lights at Dutch Henry's was much more likely to be Plover's tipster than Lew Rogan. "I'll watch out for this Luke France," Verne promised.

He went out, admitting that the case against Rogan was weakened. The main point against Rogan dissolved if Plover had said Luke instead of Lew. At the same time Verne was stubbornly determined to face Rogan with a few questions.

It was only ten in the morning and the man might still be in his room. Verne hurried down Idaho Street and went into the Central Hotel. At the lobby desk he glanced at a key rack back of it. Key number 218 was missing and key 230 was on its hook. It indicated that Canby was in his room and Rogan wasn't.

Nevertheless Verne went upstairs and moved quietly down a corridor. He passed room 218 and went on to number 230. His knock there wasn't answered. Upon trying the door, he found it locked.

He went down to the lobby and waited there a while. Rogan could be out to a late breakfast and might soon return.

Verne saw roomers come and go. The desk

194

clerk was playing cards with a drummer and usually he wasn't disturbed. An incomer merely took his key from its hook and went upstairs with it.

Why not help himself to Rogan's key and search the man's room? The idea tempted Verne. He might find evidence linking Rogan to Canby, or even to the Plover gang. Merely a memo or a name or an address might do it. And if Rogan was an errand-runner for Canby there could be some indication as to the nature of the errands.

A search of the room shouldn't take more than ten or fifteen minutes. There was a risk, but the stakes were worth it. Verne got up and crossed the lobby to a wall map of Ada County which hung near the key rack. He pretended to study the map until he was sure that the clerk was absorbed with his card game.

Then Verne Hallam deftly took key 230 from its hook and went upstairs. Room 218 was quiet as he passed it. He went on to 230, unlocked it and went in. It was unoccupied and the bed was unmade. A balcony window had its shade half drawn. Verne raised it to get better light and then began a brisk search.

A chambermaid might come in to make the bed or Rogan himself might return. Verne opened a table drawer and skimmed through a miscellany of papers there. A receipt from a Kelton hotel dated three weeks ago reminded Verne that Rogan had ridden from Utah on the stage with Nan Stanley. Other papers were equally unimportant. Verne could find nothing which pertained to Wade Canby or which might remotely connect Rogan with the outlawry of the Plover gang.

It was the same when he sifted through the contents of a top bureau drawer. A lower drawer had a loaded forty-five gun, which indicated that Rogan sometimes went about armed but wasn't armed this morning. Verne, wearing a gun himself, would be in no physical danger if the man should walk in on him.

The salt-and-pepper coat hanging from a wall peg was the one Rogan had worn on the stage trip from Kelton. Verne went through it and in an inner pocket found a small notebook. Maybe it would have an incriminating name or address or perhaps a memo of some appointment with Canby. If Rogan on the stage from Kelton had heard Nan Stanley tell Lois Lindsay about her brothers' plans—for instance that they were bringing along five thousand dollars—Rogan could have made a note of it.

Steps in the hallway alerted Verne. It could be a chambermaid or Rogan coming back, or someone coming to call on Rogan. Verne braced himself for an encounter. But the footsteps passed and went on.

The little book had too many notations to be

digested in a few minutes. So Verne put it in his pocket and quietly left the room, locking the door behind him. Down in the lobby he pretended to study the wall map for half a minute, then slipped the key back on its hook. He left the hotel fairly sure that his trespass wouldn't be suspected. When Rogan missed his notebook he'd think he'd misplaced it somewhere.

For a spot to look through it Verne picked an establishment called the Bonanza diagonally across this same corner and reputed to be Idaho's most elaborately equipped gambling house. The games didn't start till afternoon but the bar was open. Except for attendants and a few bar customers the place was empty.

"Has Lew Rogan been in this morning?" Verne asked a white-jacketed bartender.

"Rogan?" The barman cocked an eye. "Not this early. I doubt if he's even up yet."

"He was in here at ten o'clock night before last, I understand."

"I'm only the day man, so I wouldn't know. Say, Mister; you're that cowboy who shot it out with some road agents, ain'tcha?"

Verne admitted it. "What about a man named Luke France? Does he ever come in here?"

"Once in a while. Ain't seen him for a coupla days though."

"I'll rest my feet a while if you don't mind." Verne went to a wall table and sat down. There he took out Rogan's notebook and went through it, page by page.

The entries went back for more than a year. Mostly they were items of expense accounting for trips Rogan had taken. To Verne it suggested that someone else had paid those expenses. But there was no mention anywhere of Wade Canby.

There were memos giving the price-per-ounce of bar silver on certain definite days, of prices posted for gold dust at various banks, and prices quoted for various Idaho mining stocks. But there was nothing to connect Rogan with Canby or Plover, or with any known frequenter of Smeed's saloon, such as Shoop or Luke France.

On the last page of the booklet was a notation of a price paid at Kelton for a stagecoach ticket to Boise City. It was dated June 8, 1879. Right beneath this was an item which startled Verne:

John Gresham; b. Nov. 24, 1839

It was proof that Rogan had had at least a passing interest in John Gresham. Apparently the notation had been made at Kelton, just prior to Rogan's boarding the stage there. But why? And what did the initial b. stand for? It could be a birth date. But that would make Gresham only thirty-nine years old and Verne felt sure the man was past fifty.

In any case why would Rogan have the

slightest interest in the birth date of a wandering wagon driver like Gresham? Yet it had to mean something and there had to be a reason for Rogan to make a note of it.

Verne Hallam went out and began working the Idaho Street bars on a chance of seeing either Rogan or Luke France. He should be able to spot France by his long, narrow face, handlebar mustaches and flat Texas hat turned up in front—a tall gunslung man in brown corduroys.

At Verne's third inquiry he got a reaction from the barman. "Look, Mister," the saloonman advised ominously, "if I was you I'd be careful about goin' around askin' nosey questions about Luke France. He's a mean one and he's plenty gun-quick. If he hears about it he's liable to look you up and teach you to mind your own business."

"I'll bear that in mind," Verne promised.

But it gave him an idea. *Since I can't go to Luke France. I'll make him come to me.*

With that thought in mind he spent the rest of the day pointedly inquiring at bars, dice joints and billiard rooms as to the whereabouts of Luke France, and in particular as to the man's whereabouts at ten o'clock night before last.

It'll get a rise out of him, maybe, one way or another!

According to Alanson the man was a "trick shot with a six-gun." According to an Idaho

Street barman he was "a mean one and plenty gun-quick." How would such a man react when he learned that Verne Hallam had spent the day inquiring about where he'd been at the hour of a crime sixteen miles down the Overland road?

After supper Verne looked up Ben Alanson and asked that question. The deputy pondered it shrewdly. "If he's in the clear he'll likely get sore and come at you in the open. If he figures you've got something on him he'll likely come at you in the dark. Which reminds me of a gun trick he put on at a county fair exhibition last summer."

"What was that?"

"He'd do the usual stunts first, like usin' a mirror to shoot back over his shoulder. Then he'd put a bull's-eye on a wall across the stage and aim at it, tellin' his gal helper to turn out the lights. When the stage went dark he'd shoot. Then the lights would come on again and guess what."

"There'd be a bullet hole through the bull's-eye," Verne guessed.

"You said it. So better stay away from him in the dark."

It was dark when Verne left Alanson and went to see Jim Agnew. "This is confidential, Jim," he said to the liveryman. "I searched Rogan's room and found a little pocket notebook. When he was

200

in Kelton three weeks ago he wrote in it: 'John Gresham; b. Nov. 24, 1839.' Why would he do that?"

"Humph!" Agnew muttered. "That's the name of the wagon man who disappeared the other night. Rogan could've run into him at Kelton just before the Stanley boys hired him."

"Yes but why would he write down the name and put a date after it?"

"It's got me stumped, boy. If you figure it out, let me know. Right now you look kinda tuckered. Better go home and get some sleep."

It was good advice and Verne took it. In the Overland lobby he called for his key and went up to his room. After going in he closed the door behind him and groped for the room's kerosene lamp.

The lamp's glass chimney had to be removed before a wick could be lighted. As Verne's fingers touched the glass he suddenly knew that he wasn't alone—or at least that someone else had been here within the last few minutes.

For the glass lamp globe was hot—so hot that Verne had to jerk his fingers away. Not more than two minutes ago this lamp had been burning.

The window shade was drawn, shutting out starlight, and the room was quite dark. Verne moved a silent step to one side and drew his gun, standing rigidly with his back to a wall. He had the feeling that another man stood not more than ten feet away and if so he too would have a gun in his hand.

It could be Luke France, or it might be Rogan.

Had Rogan returned his call? Maybe the man knew by now that Verne Hallam had searched number 230 at the Central and was here to make a counter-search of Hallam's at the Overland. Hearing footsteps coming down the hall he would blow out the lamp, leaving the lamp chimney hot.

Or it could be France. Alanson's warning came back: "If he figures you've got something on him he'll likely come at you in the dark." A trick gunman who could hit a bull's-eye in the dark!

Verne fished a pencil from his pocket and tossed it in the direction of the lamp table. There were tinkles as the pencil landed, rolled and fell.

The sound drew no shot. Verne tried again, this time tossing a handful of matches. Again there were faint sounds of impact, but if another man was in the room he made no response.

Keeping his back to the walls Verne began circling the room quietly. When the bed stopped him he groped his way around it, always with his gun level and alert.

After covering all the wall space he concluded that the intruder had come and gone. He must have left only a minute before Verne's arrival. Cautiously Verne struck a match, his lips drooping sheepishly when he saw that he was alone.

Then he removed the warm lamp chimney and lighted the wick. Looking about for signs of a search he failed to see any. No drawers were pulled out. His saddle pack hadn't been unrolled. Apparently nothing had been disturbed.

Then he saw it! A bright, shiny 44-40 rifle cartridge on the table by the lamp. He hadn't put it there himself.

Verne picket it up and gave it a close look. The brass jacket of the shell had fresh scratches on it. A sharp steel point could have made the scratches. They spelled a name: *Hallam.*

Who had left the shell here? Rogan or France? Or could it have been Wade Canby? Clearly it was a threat and a prophesy.

A bullet with my name on it! Verne Hallam blew out the lamp, bolted his door and went to bed.

CHAPTER XVII

In his office on the second floor of the Stone Jug, Wade Canby tried restlessly to concentrate on an appraisal he was making for an Eastern capitalist. He had to get it out because he desperately needed the fifty-dollar fee. But it was hard to pin his mind on it. Four days had passed since the disappearance of John Gresham and so far searchers had failed to find his body or any proof that he was dead.

Oldham's crew had followed the tracks of two horses to running water north of Dunn's relay station and had lost them there. Canby was almost, but not quite, sure that Gil Henry had dropped the body either in deep water or into a still deeper mine shaft.

Warren Stanley had gloomily given up the search and was now at the leased valley section with his brother and sister. According to Lois, everything was going well there except for a pall of anxiety caused by the uncertain fate of John Gresham. Lois was trying to convince them that the wagoneer had gone away of his own accord, for some personal reason or because of his natural timidity. The three Stanleys were trying hard to believe it.

Gil Henry, of course, would soon be demanding

his murder money. With about as much chance of getting it, Canby thought grimly, as a snowball would have on a kitchen stove.

Canby tamped tobacco into his pipe and held a match. Then he heard heel clicks which told him that a woman was coming up the stairs from Main Street. She could be a client of any of the several lawyers on this floor.

But it was the mining engineer's office that she entered and the sight of her flabby, washed-out face gave Canby a shock. She was shabbily dressed and had a faded shawl for headgear. She closed the door and her eyes had a hard, brazen stare as she sat down to face Wade Canby.

His first shock swelled into anger. "You should know better than to come here! Right in broad daylight! Did anyone see you?"

"What if they did?" Belle Henry laid a worthless mining title on the desk. "I took it in one time for an old bar bill." Her puffy eyelid drooped in a wink. "If anyone asks, I can say I want your advice about it. What I really want, naturally, is ten thousand dollars. In cash! You've got it ready?" The Idaho City saloonwoman held out her hand.

"Keep your voice down," Canby cautioned edgily. "Of course I haven't. And why should I? I claim it wasn't Gil who did it. It was one of Plover's men. So why should I pay Gil?"

Belle's smile had ice in it. "Gil was afraid

205

you'd welsh like that. So he hasn't finished the job yet. And won't till you pony up the dough."

Canby's mouth hung open. "You mean he didn't . . ."

"I mean he's got your man alive in a safe place. He'll stay alive till you come across."

Canby felt helpless and trapped. "And if I don't?" But he could guess the answer even as he asked.

"I don't know why you want him dead," Belle said. "But it must have something to do with the tenth of July, the day you're set to get married." She paused as heavy footsteps came up the entrance stairs. The voices of two men, Judge Curtis and Governor Biggerstaff, came nearer and at the top of the stairs the two men turned down a corridor to the south wing.

Belle went on: "He must have some deadwood on you, something that would cook your goose if the lady knew about it. And believe me, Wade Canby, she'll know if you don't pay off."

Canby mopped sweat from his face and tried a bluff. "She wouldn't believe the likes of you, Belle."

"No, she wouldn't," Belle Henry admitted. "She wouldn't believe a broken-down saloonwoman like me. But she'll believe this Gresham fella, I'll bet, if she finds him on her front lawn about six hours before the wedding."

"Believe what?" Canby bluffed huskily. "What

could he say to her?" It was clear to him that Belle Henry still didn't know that Gresham was Marcus Lindsay.

"I don't know what he'd say. Maybe he wouldn't need to say anything. All I know is that he's got something on you. Something that scares the hell out of you. Want to risk it, Canby?"

Not for anything could Canby risk it. He licked his lip and tried one more avenue of evasion. "How do I know you've got him? For all I know Gil never went near him."

"Then how did he get this? Read it." Belle dropped a note on the desk. Although crumpled, it was in a dainty envelope which, by its postmarks, had been mailed at Boise City and received at Dunn's. Canby took out the enclosure and saw that it was a short, gracious thank-you note to John Gresham from Nan Stanley.

"Where else could Gil get it," Belle demanded, "except from Gresham?"

To Canby it was dismally conclusive and meant that the whip hand was Gil Henry's. "I haven't got ten thousand dollars," he said bleakly.

"Then get it! Borrow it, beg it or steal it!" Belle snapped the ultimatum and stood up. "I'm taking a room at the Central Hotel, where I can keep an eye on you. If you don't hand me the money by dark of July ninth you know what'll happen the next morning."

Canby stared helplessly as she left the office.

The clicks of her heels on the Main Street stairs were like hammers on his brain.

A morning later Verne Hallam, leading an unladen pack mare, rode his big, blue-roan gelding onto the Seventh Street ferry and crossed to the south side of the river. There he took the down-valley trail toward the Stanley place. It was the second day of July, with the air balmy. The mare, after an idle three weeks in Agnew's corral, trotted briskly along behind as though sensing she was on her way to pasture. "You'll have a chance to kick up your heels, Molly," Verne said. "No such luck for Blue and me. We've got work to do and no time to fool around."

The work was to find Gresham if he was alive and to dig up the truth about certain people, mainly Wade Canby. "It's a tight deadline, Blue. In just eight days more he's due to hitch up with a right nice lady."

He knew that the nice lady was spending the day with the Stanleys and that her boy, Mark, was with her. A boy and a farm and a bright midsummer day all went together and Lois Lindsay was going out of her way to pamper Mark these last two weeks before she'd have to leave him at home and go off on a wedding trip.

Verne's own errand today was mainly to transfer his pack mare from a livery stable to a wide green pasture. Nan and her brothers had pressed him to do so. They were also pasturing a pair of pet burros which belonged to the boy, Mark.

A farm wagon, townward bound, met and passed Verne. The farmer had his wife with him and the wagon bed was full of starched and scrubbed children. No doubt they were going in to spend the Fourth at the Capitol, when the town would stage its annual celebration with a parade and a picnic and patriotic speeches, all to the tune of bands and firecrackers. Verne wondered if the Stanleys were going in too. At Agnew's he'd heard something about Lois Lindsay and her boy driving a burro cart in the parade.

Four miles below the ferry the trail veered to the riverbank and for a hundred yards or so followed the water's edge. Cottonwood groves shaded the bottomland on either side, sometimes with willow or brierbush undergrowth. The river itself was about seventy yards in width, with slow riffles on this side and deep, still water on the other.

Verne heard first the whistle of a bullet, then the crack of a rifle. It came from a willow thicket across the river, where a smoke puff marked the spot. It was a near miss—not more than six inches from the brim of Verne Hallam's high-crowned, cream-colored hat.

His saddle scabbard had a carbine but Verne didn't draw it. There'd be nothing but a drifting smoke puff to shoot at. If he tried to ford the river and give chase he'd be at the sniper's mercy for all of the six or seven minutes it would take him to get across.

A better plan occurred to Verne and he kept riding on, just as though he hadn't heard a breath of death whistle by his head. In a moment more he was again in a screen of cottonwoods, single-footing his roan on down the river trail.

CHAPTER XVIII

The mare did kick up her heels when Verne turned her loose in the Stanley section. She galloped off to join a pair of grazing mules. "Next time you need her she'll be fat as butter," Warren Stanley said. He'd met Verne just inside the gate and they rode on to the barn together.

"You got here just at the right time," Warren said. "Nan's fryin' a pair of cockerels a neighbor sent over."

A rosy-cheeked boy came around a corner of the barn riding bareback on an elderly burro. He shouted a shrill welcome and Verne said, "Hi, cowboy."

A second burro, equally gray with age, stood sleepily in a corral.

Nan come running from the house. "We thought you'd deserted us, Verne. I bet you came just because you heard about the fried chicken."

"I came because I couldn't stay away." The way Verne said it made the girl turn and call to the boy on the burro. "Time for you to wash up, Mark."

Verne wondered why the boy would own *two* burros. One should be all he'd need to ride or play with. A little later he got the answer. Six of them were at the dining room table, Nan in a bright yellow kitchen apron proudly serving them hot biscuits and honey along with her fried-chicken dinner. Paul was there, looking fit again. "Tell Verne about the burros, Lois," he said.

"They're getting rather ancient," Lois Lindsay admitted. "Fifteen years old this summer. They were five years old when my husband used them on his last prospecting venture. I meant to get rid of them but kept putting it off. And when my little boy got big enough to play with them it was too late. They've been like members of the family ever since."

"Seem to be plenty gentle," Verne remarked.

"Like kittens," Lois agreed. "Six years ago we broke them to cart harness. Along came the Fourth of July parade with all the old-timers like John Hailey and the Chesboros and the Broadbents driving rigs in it. In memory of my husband they persuaded me to drive a cart with the two burros hitched to it. Since then it's been an annual tradition. When Mark got to be six years old he rode with me. When he was seven I let him drive. I, of course, sit by him with a watchful eye. And day after tomorrow we'll do it again."

"We're all going in to see them," Nan exclaimed gaily.

"I'll be watching myself," Verne promised.

"It may be the last year we can do it," Lois said.

"After all when donkeys get to be fifteen years old it's time for them to retire."

Verne looked at her clear strong face and his thoughts fixed upon Canby. If his suspicions were justified, what a tragedy it would be for this fine gentlewoman to marry the man! And what a calamity for the boy, Mark! Only a day and a week were left now. It made Verne restless to get away and take up the trail again—the trail of a guilt which he couldn't yet quite pin on Wade Canby.

He'd be grossly presumptuous if he broached his suspicions to this lady who expected to become the man's wife. He could theorize about Rogan and Luke France, but not about Canby.

"Paul," he ventured presently, "do you remember Floyd Plover saying 'Either you're a liar or Lew is'?"

"Sure," Paul said. "It was when he raided our camp."

"We've turned up another man who used to run with that bunch, and maybe still does. One of 'em once alibied him at a shooting trial. Name's Luke France. He's the guy who helped Shoop get away by shooting out the lights."

"Shoop was the guy with the red-stubbled face at Dutch Henry's?"

"That's the one. So maybe what Plover really said was, 'Either you're a liar or Luke is.' What do you think?"

Paul looked askance at his brother. After mulling it over neither of them could be sure.

Later, as he was saddling up at the barn, Verne showed them the rifle cartridge with his name scratched on it. "It's a promise somebody made me the other night. He tried to make good on it as I rode down the river this morning. So I figure to ride back another way."

Nan waved from the yard gate as he rode off. "See you in town day after tomorrow," Verne called to her. She'd promised to watch the parade with him from the steps of the Overland Hotel.

He single-footed out of the barnyard and when he was a mile beyond the pasture gate he left the trail and cut through a bottomland grove to the river. "Here's where we get wet, Blue."

Crossing wasn't difficult because most of the way the riffles were less than stirrup deep. Only for about ten yards near the north shore did the roan have to swim. The horse scrambled out on the muddy bank, blowing and shaking its hide. Verne, wet to the thighs, found a sunny spot and dismounted. He took off his boots to empty the water from them.

Drying himself in the sun he looked speculatively up river. "He knew we were taking that mare to the Stanley's. So he can count on us coming back in the afternoon. Might be he's layin' for us again."

This side of the river, like the other, had a belt

of timber along it. But on this side there was no trail and Verne had to pick his way through the shore trees. Coming down river this morning he'd spotted a landmark, a tall dead snag, close to the willow patch from which the sniper had fired. It was the only place opposite the exposed stretch of road on the other side of the river.

As he neared the snag Verne dismounted and took his carbine from its scabbard. He tied the roan and went on foot, advancing silently through the trees.

At the base of the tall dead snag he found himself in a deserted grove. Here the cottonwoods were huge and there was no underbrush. To Verne's right a line of low willows marked the water's edge but he could see no sign of life in them.

Then Verne saw fresh hoofprints. They led both ways, to and from the water-edge willows. After a moment's thought Verne followed them, not toward but away from the river. They led him to a sandy wash where an overflow from floods had cut an inland channel. It was about seven feet deep and now dry. In its bed stood a saddled horse, tethered. The saddle had an empty scabbard.

This morning, Verne concluded, the sniper had ridden to the river to pick his spot, then he'd ridden to this wash to hide his mount. Looking closely at the sandy sod Verne now made out dim footprints. After hiding his horse the man had walked back to the river, rifle in hand and treading lightly.

Since he hadn't returned he was still there.

Treading lightly himself, Verne moved that way. The water-edge willows made a dense tangle and he was within twenty steps of them before he saw the back of a crouching man. The man had a rifle and was gazing across the river.

"Waiting for somebody?"

Verne's challenge made the man straighten up. He whirled about, firing as he whirled. It was a snap shot flustered by panic and Verne's bullet, half a second late, was better aimed. It made the man stagger, floundering in a mesh of willow branches. As he reeled backward he fired again, wildly and almost straight upward.

"I'd rather not kill you," Verne said. "Better give up. There's a shell in my gun, too, and this time it's got *your* name on it."

The man dropped his rifle and came stumbling out of the willows. Blood from a scalp wound ran down his long lean face to handle-bar mustaches. "Get me to a doctor, damn you!"

"As quick as I can, Mr. Luke France," Verne promised. "Who hired you? Canby or Rogan?"

"Canby? I don't even know him. Or Rogan either. Get me a doctor before I . . ." Luke France stumbled to his knees, then collapsed face down on the sand.

Verne took his holster gun and went into the willows for the rifle. "Now I'll fetch the horses and take you to town."

It was sundown when Verne got him to the county jail. Alanson helped him put Luke France on a cell cot. Doctor Eph Smith came promptly and while he worked on the prisoner Verne gave the facts of the ambush to Alanson, showing the deputy a scratched cartridge. "He warned me with it, Ben."

"My hunch is he's telling the truth," Alanson concluded. "I mean about having no connection with Canby or Rogan. We've always had him pegged as a Plover heeler. The way I dope it, Plover gave orders to get you right after you fouled him up at Indian Creek. Top of that, you're a star witness against those five birds Robbins is chasin'. Top of *that,* you made Luke mad by asking around town where he was at the time Gresham was killed or kidnapped. So he laid for you down the river."

"But why," Verne puzzled, "would he warn me with a scratched cartridge?"

"He's a showman, remember? A trick-shot showman. The whole play fits him like a glove, but it doesn't fit Canby or Rogan."

As he went out Verne had to admit it. Certainly the last few days had added nothing to his case against Rogan and Canby. In these last days

217

Rogan had spent his time in bars and pool parlors, running no errands for Wade Canby. Canby was keeping regular hours at his office and after hours was mixing with the best people. Twice this week he'd taken his fiancée out to dinner and once the two had driven out to watch a guard-mount ceremony at Fort Boise.

But there was a solid link between Rogan and the missing Gresham. It was Gresham's name, followed by a date, scribbled in Rogan's memo book. As yet Verne hadn't questioned Rogan about it for two reasons: He didn't want to admit he'd searched the man's room or put him on guard in case the notation was a clue to Gresham's disappearance.

That night Verne slept restlessly and by morning had decided to push both Luke France and Wade Canby out of his mind and focus on Rogan. Gresham's name in the notebook implicated only Rogan. Verne had heard talk about Rogan's past in Idaho City, where long ago he'd been fired from his police job on suspicion of taking a bribe.

Wandering from bar to bar all through the day and evening of July third, Verne Hallam inquired further about that incident. Only rarely could he find anyone who'd been around long enough to have more than hearsay knowledge of it.

"It was twelve years ago," Lemp's barman told him. "They claim he let a prisoner fly the coop for a cash price. Nobody could ever prove it. Them were wild and woolly days at Idaho City and you can hear most anything you want about 'em. Wade Canby? Yeh, he lived there too about that time. I've even heard whispers about him but I never believed 'em."

"About what?"

"About bogus dust. Lots of it was passed in them days. Anybody was likely to be suspected of havin' it, or tryin' to get rid of it. They was a crew of vigilantes workin' on it and they hanged a few passers over at Wahoe Ferry. Most anybody was likely to be searched to see if he had any bogus on him. I heard they even searched Wade Canby's house one time but they didn't find any in it. Old-timer named Earnshaw was in here once gassin' about it. Claimed he was on that vigilante committee, twelve years ago."

A man came in and approached Verne. "Remember me? I'm night man at Agnew's barn."

"I remember you," Verne said.

"I hear you've been askin' around where Luke France was at ten o'clock the night that Gresham disappeared from a trail camp down by Dunn's station."

"That's right."

"Well, you don't need to ask any more. At ten that night Luke France rode into my barn and turned in a saddle horse he'd rented. I made an entry in the night book and it shows the day and hour."

That cleared Luke France from the assault on Gresham. Verne lost all interest in him and turned back to the bartender. "Where could I find that old-timer you mentioned, Earnshaw?"

"He's whackin' a bull team now and is likely to be out on the road somewhere." The barman thought a minute, then added brightly: "Tell you what. There'll be a lot of old-timers in the parade tomorrow. You can latch onto one of 'em and he'll talk your head off, if you give him a chance, about the old vigilante days."

"Thanks." It reminded Verne that he had a date with Nan tomorrow, to watch the parade with her from the steps of the Overland Hotel.

CHAPTER XIX

Except for the band music, the parade was rather dull. The Capital Band came first, followed by a column of cavalry from Fort Boise. Next came a score of mounted cowboys in column of twos, shooting guns in the air, and after them a dozen covered wagons drawn by ox teams and driven by bearded pioneers. A fife-and-drum corps marched next, and after it came an artillery cannon with a pretty girl draped in an American flag seated on it. There were the usual dignitaries: Governor Biggerstaff, Marshal Chase, the commandant at Fort Boise, Sheriff Oldham. The absence of Deputy U. S. Marshal Orlando Robbins reminded Verne that he was still off with a posse chasing five outlaw killers.

Indians came next in feathered headdresses and riding bareback on calico ponies. Boys on the walk threw firecrackers into the street and there were a few runaways.

Verne, standing by Nan on the Overland porch, watched a line of carriages pass, each containing pioneers who'd been here since the gold-boom days of the Sixties: The Durells, the Wilcoms, the Haileys, the Milton Kellys, the Bilikes, the Griffins and the Gilmores. "They'll all go to the picnic grounds," Nan chattered, "right after the parade."

Then came a hay wagon used as a float to support a pair of prospectors panning gravel, and next a military band from Fort Boise.

"Look, there come Lois and Mark!" Nan exclaimed delightedly. Two hoary burros were plodding up the street pulling a dogcart. The nine-year-old boy proudly held the reins with his mother beside him.

"Looks like they're about to play out on you, Lois," a man on the walk yelled.

"Don't let 'em run away, boy," another shouted.

Mark Lindsay flapped his reins. "Get up, Tom," he coaxed. "Move along, Jerry."

"Did you hear that, Nan?" The girl felt Verne's hand tighten on her arm.

"Hear what?"

"What he called those donkeys." Verne's eyes searched the porch and at the far end of it saw Warren Stanley in the company of a young army girl. "Wait here a minute, Nan. I'll be right back."

Verne hurried down the porch and drew Warren aside. "Listen, Warren. That mule team of yours. What's their names?"

Warren looked at him blankly. "Names? Come to think of it, I don't really know. We bought that span of mules at Kelton the day we left there. After that nobody handled 'em except John Gresham."

"If Gresham drove them for three weeks he must've called 'em something."

"Likely he did. A wagon driver generally does. I was busy prodding the cows along and never paid any attention."

"*I* did," Verne said. "Yes, he made up names for 'em all right. Thanks."

Verne rushed back to Nan, took her arm and hustled her into the Overland lobby. To her complete confusion he hurried her across the lobby and out the Main Street door. "Where on earth are you taking me, Verne Hallam?"

"Tell you on the way there. Something big just popped."

"On the way where?"

"To the cemetery. I've no idea where it is. There's a hack. We can ask the driver."

"Have you gone stark mad?" Nan demanded.

Verne had her arm and was propelling her along to a two-horse hack in mid-block. The hackman, who'd seen too many Fourth of July parades to be excited by this one, was standing by to pick up fares to the picnic grounds when the parade was over.

Verne put Nan in the cab. "Take us to the cemetery, driver."

The hackman gaped. "You mean the picnic grounds, don'tcha?"

"I mean the cemetery—the place where they bury people."

Verne got in with Nan and the cab rolled away, detouring the parade crowds. It struck Idaho Street at Sixth and turned east along it. "Tom and Jerry!" Verne exclaimed. "That's what the boy called 'em. The burros!"

"The burros? I don't see what . . ."

"They were his father's burros before Mark was born. So it was his father who named them Tom and Jerry."

"Why shouldn't he?"

"No reason at all. That was more than ten years ago. Four weeks ago a man named Gresham was given two mules to drive. He made up names for them. Names that popped naturally into his mind. I was there when he drove his wagon out of camp one morning and I heard him say: 'Get up, Tom; move along, Jerry.'"

Nan began to see what he meant but couldn't accept it. "It's just a coincidence, Verne."

"Maybe. But there's a way to check it. A sure way. Look." He took Rogan's notebook from his pocket and showed the girl a name and a date written in it.

John Gresham; b. Nov. 24, 1839

"Marcus Lindsay's headstone ought to have dates on it—a birth date and a death date. Let's take a look."

"It's too utterly wild, Verne! Are you trying to

tell us that Mark's father is still living? And that his name is John Gresham?"

"I'm not telling you anything. If there's anything to tell it'll be carved on the headstone."

The hack had reached the corner of C Street and Warm Springs Avenue, where it was turning left through an opening in a picket fence. "Here we are," the driver announced.

He stopped on a gravel roadway with rows of graves on either side. Some of the graves had marble or granite headstones. Most of them merely had headboards or wooden crosses.

Verne helped Nan out and spoke to the driver. "We're looking for the grave of a man buried ten years ago. Where's it most likely to be?"

The hackman motioned with his whip toward the left. "That there's the oldest section. They didn't start usin' the other side till about '74."

"Wait here." Verne took Nan along a path to the left. Most of the plots were shabbily kept. A few had trimmed grass and signs of attention. Here and there was a shade tree or flowering bush.

"We can pass up the weedy ones," Verne said. "If I know Mrs. Lindsay she'd put up a stone of some kind. You take that row and I'll take this one. If you see the name Lindsay, call me."

He followed a row of plots till a fence stopped him, then turned back on the adjacent row. About fifty steps away Nan was doing the same. Names on some of the headboards were faded beyond recognition. On stones they were chiseled and easily read.

Verne was on his fifth row when Nan called him. He ran to her and they stood by a slab of marble with lilac bushes about it. The inscription read:

MARCUS LINDSAY
born Nov. 24, 1839
died May 23, 1869

Nan looked at it a long solemn time before her eyes raised to meet Verne's. "Are you convinced?" he asked her.

"Almost," she said.

"Why almost?" Verne challenged. Again he showed her the notation in Rogan's book, which gave the same birth date. "What more do you want? Gresham is Lindsay and Lois has never been a widow."

"I'd believe that," Nan said, "if I could be sure that Rogan didn't do just what we've done. Maybe he suspected that Gresham is Lindsay except that he seemed too old. So he came to this grave to make a note of the birth date. If he did that, it doesn't prove a thing."

"By itself it doesn't," Verne admitted. "But it's not by itself. Gresham called two mules by the names of Lindsay's burros. Don't forget that Gresham seemed nervous and timid about coming to Boise City. The nearer he got the more scared he got. Which would be the case if he knew he had a wife here—a wife who thought he was dead."

"But why wouldn't he want to see her?"

"Maybe he *did* want to see her, but didn't want her to see him. You never saw him yourself, Nan, so you don't know how disfigured he is—burned and powder-pitted. Women turn away when he comes into a room. And don't forget it was a powder blast that killed Lindsay, if he's dead. Everything fits."

"It would explain," Nan admitted, "why he disappeared at the last camp before getting here. Maybe he was afraid his wife would see and know him, so he just . . ."

"So he just ducked out. Let's hope it was that way, Nan. But maybe he was hepped off into the woods and shot. Maybe by a Plover man, for revenge—or maybe by someone with a heap better reason than just to get even."

"Who could that be?" Nan wondered.

Verne's eyes narrowed. "Who stands most to lose if Marcus Lindsay gets to town and is recognized? What about the man who's about to marry Lindsay's wife?"

The inference shocked Nan. "You mean Mr. Canby? You think he . . ."

"I think Rogan found out at Kelton the date of Gresham's birth and made a note of it. He came here and told Canby. Canby checks the date and figures just like we do, that Gresham's Lindsay. So he sets devilment afoot to keep Gresham from ever showing up."

The girl shivered. "What shall we do? Should we tell Lois?"

Verne walked her back to the cab. "She has to be told, of course. But let's wait till we know for sure whether her husband's alive or dead. First I'll find Rogan and rattle his teeth. Maybe I can make him tell how he came to write down that birth date."

"What frightens *me,*" Nan said, "is the wedding date. It's only six days away, Verne. How can we let Lois go ahead with the preparations, seeing Canby every day if . . . ?"

"If he has just murdered her husband?" Verne supplied bluntly.

Again Nan shuddered. "Or if her husband's still living! No, Verne, we must tell her right away. Just think! The parade's over. Which means that she and Mark are down at the picnic grounds sharing a basket lunch with Canby—accepting his attentions! It's an impossible situation and we just can't let it go on."

They got back into the hack and were driven back toward the downtown district. Nan was probably right, Verne thought. It was a delicate situation and one on which a girl's judgment was likely to be better than his own.

"Suppose we do this, Nan. You give me twenty-four hours to make this case a little tighter. Then you and Warren go to some old friend of Mrs. Lindsay's, someone who knew her and her husband in the old days. Tell him everything we know and let *him* tell Lois Lindsay."

"That's exactly what we should do," Nan agreed. "I won't say a thing till this time tomorrow—I wonder what's stopping us."

The hack had arrived at Seventh Street where an excited, noisy crowd blocked the way. Verne put his head out of the hack window and called to the driver, "What's holding us up?"

"It ain't the parade," the hackman said. "It's Orlando Robbins and his posse. They're just back from Bruneau Crik and they've got them five killers they've been chasin'. Orlando's bringin' back one of his own deputies too, and he's dead. A kid named Bud Akins. It's got everybody steamed up and the whole parade crowd's follerin' along to the jail. Wouldn't surprise me much if they snatched them five killers outa jail before mornin' and strung 'em up."

CHAPTER XX

Once again Verne Hallam knocked at the door of room 230. It was his third call here at the Central Hotel since leaving Nan with her brother at the Overland. He was determined to find Lew Rogan and make him explain the notebook entry.

Again there was no answer. The door was locked. Yet Rogan was in town and he wasn't hiding. He'd been in the parade crowd this morning. Later he'd been seen at the picnic grounds where several hundred people were now assembled.

Verne left the door of room 230 and started toward the head of the stairs. He passed Canby's room and assumed the man wasn't in because only an hour ago Verne had seen him at the picnic grounds in company with Lois and Mark. Verne hadn't intruded himself but instead had hurried back up to Idaho Street to resume his search for Rogan.

Now, from beyond a door near the head of the stairs, he heard voices and one of them was familiar. It wasn't Rogan's. Alertly Verne stopped to listen. A man and a woman in the room were talking in undertones. The man, he presently concluded, was Wade Canby.

Why would Canby so abruptly leave his

fiancée at a picnic celebration and come here to see another woman? Clearly it was a business discussion. The man's voice was querulous—the woman's hard, cold, unyielding.

The pitch of the tones raised a little and Verne caught words from Canby. *"You've got to give me more time!"*

"Only till sundown of the ninth," the woman said.

The voices lowered and Verne heard not a word more. A chair scraped as the man got up to leave. Not to be caught eavesdropping, Verne noted the room's number and went quickly down to the lobby. He slipped into the bar and from it saw Wade Canby come down the stairs and go out to the street. His face had the look of a man who has just come off second best in an argument.

When the lobby desk was deserted a few minutes later, Verne took a look at the registry book. The woman's room was number 200. Thumbing back to the last registration for that room he found the name, Belle Plover of Idaho City. She'd signed in three days ago and was credited with having paid a week's room rent in advance.

To get her pedigree Verne hurried to the county jail to see Sheriff Oldham.

Oldham barely heard his question. "We got troubles of our own, Hallam. Look out there!"

231

Beyond a grilled window, on Eighth Street, Verne saw more than a hundred noisy men milling about. As many more were assembled in front of the jail's Idaho Street entrance. Deputy Ben Alanson and City Marshal Paxton, riot guns in hand, were looking grimly out at them.

"Orlando Robbins's crew will be here to side us as soon as they get some rest," Oldham said. "They've been in the saddle for a week and are about played out. It's not likely to get rough till after dark. But that crowd's been lapping up Fourth-of-July whisky ever since breakfast. They'd like to wind up the celebration with a big necktie party."

The five outlaws brought in by the Robbins posse—Hugo, Joad, Webber, Shoop and Schulte—were all in the same cell and Verne went back for a look at them. He recognized one of them as the man who'd posed as Bob Baker. On a cot in the next cell, with his head bandaged, lay Luke France.

Back in the front office Verne again asked his question: "Who's Belle Plover?"

"She runs a bar in the next county north of here," Oldham said. "Belle's Floyd Plover's widow and she's got three no-good brothers. You met one of them—Dutch Henry."

"Who are the other two?"

"Gabe and Gil. Gabe was run out of Idaho twelve years ago and hasn't been seen since. Last we heard of Gil was a year ago when he killed a man in Montana and lit out for who-knows-where. We've got a poster about him on file."

"Belle's at the Central Hotel," Verne said. "Wade Canby called at her room just now and I heard him say 'I've got to have more time.' What could he mean by that?"

The Ada County sheriff shrugged. "She's lived in Idaho City for fourteen years. Anyone who's been in business there that long's bound to have an old mining title or two. Canby's a mining engineer and broker. It's likely she wants him to sell a claim for her, or maybe dig up a backer to operate it for her, but he says it'll take time." Oldham crossed to an Idaho Street window and stood scowling out at the crowd.

The answer didn't impress Verne. He had a feeling that Canby, and not the woman, had been the petitioner in room 200. Her tone had indicated that she held the whip hand.

"Blast those bums out there!" Oldham fretted. "I've half a mind to wake up the Robbins crew right now. But I promised 'em seven hours sleep. Look, cowboy, what about you taking an emergency deputyship till things quiet down?" He took a badge from a table drawer and held it in his open palm.

Verne was about to say No when it occurred to him that a badge might give him some leverage over Rogan. The man might be more easily cowed by a law officer than by a civilian without authority.

"I'll take it on one condition, Sheriff—that you let me shake down Lew Rogan first. I've got reason to think he's mixed up in the disappearance of that wagoneer, Gresham. Found a notebook in his room with Gresham's name in it. If he won't say why, I'd like to pick him up on suspicion and hold him in jail overnight. How about it?"

The sheriff pursed his lips thoughtfully, then nodded. "You can have till dark to work Rogan over. I don't look for anything but loud talk before then. Soon as it's dark I want you here to help us stand off those street rowdies. Here you are. Pin it on and consider yourself sworn in." He tossed the brass badge and Verne caught it.

Verne Hallam pinned the badge on his shirt and went out the Eighth Street exit. He stood on the walk there only long enough to make sure that Rogan wasn't in the street crowd, then he rounded the corner and made the same inspection on the Idaho Street side. Rogan wasn't in sight. The crowd was ugly but not ready for action—yet. Clearly it lacked a leader. It had formed spontaneously largely on account of the extreme youth and popularity of the two murdered deputies, Chuck Prather and Bud Akins.

Verne shouldered his way down the walk to Seventh and went into the Central Hotel. "Has

Lew Rogan come in yet?" he asked the desk clerk.

"Yep, he's come and gone. I just saw him go into the Empire Billiard Hall across the street. Shoots a slick cue, Lew does. Likely you'll find him trimmin' a sucker over there."

Verne went out and crossed to the billiard hall. Its owner stood behind a cigar counter and two customers were playing pool at the front table. The other tables were unoccupied except one at the extreme rear where Lew Rogan was practising carom shots all alone.

"Want me to rustle up a game for you, Mister?" the owner offered. "I can take you on myself if you like. Business is dull right now 'cause everybody wants to see what's goin' on up at the jail."

"No thanks." As Verne walked toward the rear he opened his jacket a little to let the badge show on his shirt. Rogan, making a difficult billiard shot, didn't see him at once.

"Let's talk about John Gresham," Verne said bluntly.

Rogan straightened up. He turned his fleshy, unshaven face toward Verne and then let his eyes drop to the brass badge. "Gresham?" he asked cautiously. "Who's he?"

"You ought to know, Rogan. You wrote down his name and the date of his birth." Verne took the notebook from his pocket and flashed it in front of Rogan's eyes.

"So it was you who stole it!" The man's tone was a hoarse bluster but the eyes had fear in them. "You got no right to prowl my room. I could have you pinched."

Verne saw that he wasn't armed. "Let's talk about Gresham," he insisted. "They're looking for his body in the woods above Dunn's station. So far you're the only suspect we've got, Rogan."

The unkempt face paled a little. "Me? Why me? I never had anything to do with him."

"Except to write his name in a book and go to the trouble of looking up his birthday. I'll give you one minute to say why, Rogan. If you don't, I'll have to toss you in jail along with five of your friends."

"Friends? What friends?"

"The ones you passed along a five-thousand-dollar tip to. Floyd Plover named you when he raided a trail camp the night he was shot by Gresham. 'Either you're a liar,' he said, 'or Lew is.'"

"He meant some other Lew, not me!"

"But you're the only Lew we can lay hands on right now. And you're the only Lew who kept Gresham's name in a little black book. The minute's up. So come along to jail. You won't like it up there. A noisy crowd's out in front and they've got ropes."

"They wouldn't touch me!" Rogan said hoarsely.

"Let's hope not. But of course with six of you in the same cell they might make a mistake and take out the wrong five. Tell the truth about that name and date and maybe I'll let you have a cell all by yourself."

"All right. I'll tell you." Rogan came a step closer, looking furtively toward the front where the shop's owner and two pool players were paying no attention to the rear of the room. Verne saw Rogan change ends with his grip on the billiard cue but didn't realize why till it was too late. "This Gresham came up to me at Kelton and . . ."

The big end of the billiard cue was loaded with lead to give it weight. Rogan, holding the small end, swished the cue through the air and brought the butt crashing down on Verne's head.

Verne's knees gave way under him and his mind went blank. When the owner rushed back there he found the deputy sheriff senseless on the floor. Rogan had scurried out a rear door to an alley. "Hey!" the owner yelled to his pool customers. "One of you fellas go fetch Doc Eph Smith."

CHAPTER XXI

When Verne came to consciousness two men were standing by him. He was in bed in his room at the Overland and the grayness at the window meant it was twilight outside. Except for an aching head he felt no great discomfort. The man at his right was Eph Smith and the other was Deputy Ben Alanson.

The doctor grinned cheerfully. "Welcome back, boy. We thought at first it might be a concussion. Turns out you've got nothing but a lump on the noggin. A good night's sleep'll put you on your feet again."

He'd been clubbed by Rogan, Verne remembered. The thought made him try to get out of bed but Alanson pressed him down. "Don't fret about Rogan, fella. Three witnesses saw him bean you. Another saw him grab a horse in the alley. Last seen he was high-tailin' toward Middleton."

He assured Verne that there wasn't a chance for Rogan to get away. Hard-riding men were hot after him. "What made him sock you, Hallam?"

When Verne had fully collected his wits he summarized the words he'd exchanged with Rogan. "I must've hit close to the mark to make him crack down on me like that."

"What stampeded him," Alanson concluded,

"was your saying you'd toss him in a cell with Hugo and company. You can't blame him either. Not with a liquored-up lynch mob milling around the jail. But we can handle it. Orlando Robbins and his crew are there now to back us up. See you tomorrow, cowboy."

As the deputy went out a waitress came in with hot broth which the doctor had ordered sent up. "Soon as you finish it, I'll give you a sedative," Eph Smith said.

He went down the hall to look in on another patient. The waitress propped Verne up and put the tray across his knees. "Are Warren Stanley and his sister here?" Verne asked her.

"No," she told him. "They drove back to their farm, but they said they'll be in town again tomorrow."

To Verne it meant that they wanted to consult Paul as to the when and how of telling Lois Lindsay about the identity of John Gresham. He felt certain that they hadn't yet heard about his own encounter with Rogan.

Eph Smith returned briskly and gave his patient two capsules. Verne swallowed them, finished his broth and the waitress took away the tray. "I want you to stay in bed till morning," the doctor ordered. He too left the room and Verne heard him go down the lobby stairs.

I'll lie here just half an hour, Verne decided. *Then I'll get up and go see Belle Plover. Got to find out what she's cooking up with Canby. Or maybe I ought to see Canby first. He says he's got to have more time. Time for what?*

Verne lay there debating in his mind which to tackle first, the man or the woman. He needn't bother about Rogan. Rogan was on the run and sure to be caught. The thing now was to nail down the case against Canby. Time was running out. The man's marriage was set for the tenth and the Plover woman mentioned "sundown of the ninth." The wedding eve! Could Belle tell tales on Canby? Was she demanding a pay-off?

Verne Hallam's senses thickened so gradually that he wasn't aware of it. He had no way of knowing that Eph Smith had doubled the sedative, giving two capsules instead of the usual one. He couldn't know that the doctor was admitting it at this very minute, to a crony at the Overland bar. "The boy's itching to get up and go gunning for trouble again," he chuckled, "so I slipped him a sleep dose. Come morning he'll be on his own again, good as new."

When Verne awakened there was light at his window. It wasn't gray dawn but the rosier light that comes between daybreak and sunrise. He'd slept like the dead for nine hours.

Nine wasted hours, he thought remorsefully as he got out of bed. He dressed and washed but didn't take time to shave. He must make up for those wasted hours.

Buckling on his gunbelt he hurried downstairs. The dining room had just opened and an early breakfaster was in there. It reminded Verne that he'd had nothing except a bowl of broth since noon yesterday.

The early breakfaster was Jim Agnew and Verne joined him. "Hear you got conked with a pool cue," the liveryman grinned. "How you feelin' now?"

"I can get around." Impatiently Verne beckoned a waitress. "Ham and scrambled, please." A coffee pot was on the table and he filled a cup.

"You missed a big show last night," Agnew told him. "Biggest blow-up this town ever had."

"You mean that lynch mob? It raided the jail?"

"Nope. But it was nip-and-tuck for a while. Kept all of Oldham's crew and all of Robbins's crew up all night, standin' 'em off. They had to recruit both the town constables and three or four ex-deputies."

"Any shooting?"

"Not a shot fired except straight up into the air, like always on the Fourth of July. But they tossed a dozen or so smoke bombs through the jail windows and like to smoked the jail crew out. At least five hundred would-be lynchers in the streets and most of them drunk. It like to scared the gizzards out of the five guys they wanted to string up. But that wasn't the worst of it."

"What was worse?" Verne prompted.

Agnew waited till the girl had served Verne before answering. "Calling all peace officers and ex-peace officers to help defend the jail saved five no-good necks, but it left the town wide open for strong-armers. So there were a few footpad jobs pulled off down along Idaho Street. And one cold murder."

"Yeh? Who got murdered?"

"Ross Jackson, cashier at the Bonanza gambling hall. His guard, Vint Nash, usually sits by while he handles the night's take. But Vint used to be a county deputy and just before midnight, when it looked like the jail was going to be crashed, he was called up there to help Oldham and Robbins. Purty near all the Bonanza customers went up there too, to see the finish. The place was nearly empty when the bartender heard the shot."

"A shot from the cashier's office?"

"That's where. Ross Jackson was dead when they went in there. Whoever shot him had grabbed all the money in sight and got out the back way. Fourteen thousand in cash."

Other matters weighed heavier on Verne's mind. "Any word from Rogan?"

"Only that they're hard on his heels somewhere near Middleton."

Verne wolfed his food and hurried out to the street. It was oddly quiet after a riotous night, the walks littered with empty six-gun shells and half-burned firecrackers.

Up at the jail corner, only a scattering of broken bottles and a sleeping drunk were left to show of last night's siege.

From that corner Verne hurried a block east to Seventh and Idaho. The pool hall was locked and so too was the Bonanza where a man had been murdered only seven hours ago.

The Central Hotel's proprietor, Gale Gibbs, was at the lobby desk when Verne went in. "Is Wade Canby in his room?"

"Reckon so," the hotel man said sleepily. His eyes looked like he'd been up all night, missing none of the excitement. "He came in a little after midnight and hasn't come down yet this morning."

"What about Mrs. Plover?"

"Belle? She checked out about twenty minutes ago and caught the stage for Idaho City."

"The devil she did! Had she planned on going this morning?"

"Nope. Fact is she paid her room rent a week in advance and it still had three days to go. She didn't ask for a refund either. If you want to see Wade Canby, here he comes now."

The mining engineer came down the stairs and went into the dining room for breakfast. Verne promptly followed and took a seat opposite him.

"Howdy, Hallam." Canby spoke with a stiff cordiality. "Heard you ran into some grief yesterday. Glad to see you up and around."

Verne went straight to his point. "I'm looking for a woman named Belle Plover. They say she just checked out. Know her?"

"How could I help it?" Canby answered with a shrug. "I used to live in the next county north and Belle's quite a character up there. Fact is she's a client of mine. Came into my office the other day and wanted my advice about an old mining title she'd picked up. Left it with me." The engineer smiled cynically. "She probably won it in a crap game and it's not worth the paper it's written on. I was planning to hand it back to her this morning. You say she checked out?"

"According to the hotel man, she has."

Canby grimaced. "Then I'll have to mail it to her." From an inside pocket he brought a mining claim patent and it seemed to confirm his alleged connection with Belle Plover and to dismiss it as of no consequence. "It's the old Flying Dutchman claim. Hasn't been worth working for ten years."

Verne had heard enough to make him sure of two things: that advice about a mine claim was merely a cover-up for the real issue between the woman and Canby, and that whatever the real issue was, it had somehow been settled during the night just past, allowing the Idaho City woman to catch a daybreak stage for home.

At midnight there'd been a murder diagonally across from this hotel. A few minutes after the murder Wade Canby had come in and gone up to his room. And six hours later Belle Henry Plover, her mission possibly accomplished, had left by stage for home. If there was a connection between the three events Canby certainly wouldn't admit it. Questions would merely put him on guard. The person to question, Verne decided, was Belle Plover.

To disarm suspicion and make himself plausible Verne said: "I'm working on the Gresham case. Oldham made me a deputy yesterday and I thought I'd begin with Belle Plover."

"What," Canby asked with an air of detachment, "could *she* know about it?"

"Probably nothing," Verne said. "But it might be she sicked a gunman on Gresham. He shotgunned her husband down at Glenn's Ferry. Just thought I'd ask her how she feels about it. As good a starting point as any. Well, so long, Canby."

Verne got up and left the hotel, fairly sure he hadn't put Canby on his guard. *The guy's a plain and fancy liar,* Verne thought as he walked toward Agnew's stable.

The only thing that seemed to make sense was that the woman had something on Canby and had come down here demanding a pay-off. He'd begged for more time in which to raise the money but she'd given him only till the wedding eve. Desperate, he could have raised the money last night by robbing the Bonanza cashier, taking advantage of the diversion caused by the riot a block up the street. It would give him the cash needed to pay off the Plover woman.

Maybe it was that way and maybe it wasn't. If it was, the woman had the money with her right now as she rode the stage coach toward the next county seat north. Catching her with it would convict both her and Canby.

Convicting Canby would stop Lois from keeping her wedding date with him, whether or not John Gresham was still alive.

"Saddle a remount for me, Jim," Verne said at the livery barn. "I'll ride my roan and lead the extra horse, for speed. Got to make Idaho City by sundown."

It was a rough thirty-five miles, up Cottonwood Gulch, over Shaw's Mountain Pass and down Robie Creek, then down one fork of More's Creek and up another. Verne changed his saddle from horse to horse every five miles but he couldn't change his own weary legs.

He was aching in every joint when at noon he came to Anderson's Halfway House, where the daily stage changed teams. Verne gulped a plate of beef and potatoes while they grained his mounts. "How far am I behind the northbound stage?"

"About forty minutes," they told him.

It meant he wasn't gaining. The stage had four

horses, which much of the time would be kept at a run. A saddle horse could hardly catch up with it in the remaining seventeen miles.

Verne spurred on between steep, piney slopes, leading his remount, crossing and recrossing the swift clear riffles of More's Creek. He was changing horses when a southbound wagoneer passed him. The stage, he learned, was still nearly an hour ahead.

The sun was low when he next shifted the saddle. And it had dropped completely behind a timbered skyline when he came out of the canyon into a wide, open basin where myriad mounds of gravel were heaped along the stream banks. Goldseekers, during the Sixties, had panned many fortunes here. The huddle of drab frame buildings at the basin's center was sure to be Idaho City. From here it looked lifeless, but as a county seat it should have a sheriff and a jail. Verne took the deputy's badge from his shirt and pinned it on the lapel of his coat.

He reined into the town's dusty street and stopped at a false-fronted livery stable. A denim-clad hostler was chewing a straw by the door. "I watered 'em at the creek," Verne said. "Soon as they stop blowing give 'em a forkful of hay and a rubdown."

The man's gaze fixed with respect on the brass badge. "You from Ada County?" he asked as he unsaddled the roan.

Verne nodded, then motioned toward the stage coach parked in the wagon yard. "When did it get in? The stage from Boise City?"

"About an hour ago. This is as fur as it goes. Starts back at seven in the mornin'."

"Was Belle Plover on it?"

"Yep." The hostler pointed down the shabby street. "That's her saloon right the other side of the hotel."

"Is she there now?"

"Nope. She rented a rig and took off up the Pioneerville trail."

"What for?"

"Search me. Went after a load of hooch, maybe. They say she buys her likker from a still in the hills."

"Isn't that against the law?"

"Agin federal law, maybe. But not agin county law. Sheriff here's got all he can do crackin' down on claim jumpers and stoppin' a saloon brawl now and then. Let the government revenuers do the fussin' with moonshiners, Ike says."

"Where is he now? The sheriff?"

"About this time of day you'll find him on the hotel porch with his feet on the rail. He'll be waitin' for the supper bell. Never misses a meal, Ike don't."

Verne found the man in exactly that pose. County Sheriff Ike Billings had a two-hundred-and-sixty-pound build, mostly telescoped between short fat legs and three meaty chins. The chins were resting on his chest and his eyes were napping when Verne spoke to him. "Hallam's my name. I'm an Ada County deputy and I need your help."

The eyes came open but the boots stayed on the porch rail and the hands remained clasped over the paunch. "Help? What about?"

"The Bonanza at Boise City was robbed last night and the cashier murdered."

"Yeh, the stage driver told me about it. What makes you think the killer came this way?"

"I don't. But I suspect he passed all or part of the money to Belle Plover and she brought it with her on the stage."

Still the legs remained horizontal and the hands clasped over the midriff bulge. "You got anything to back it up?"

"Nothing definite," Verne admitted. "Just a hunch."

"You mean you've got no warrant?"

"I haven't any warrant. All I've got's an Ada County badge and a hunch that Belle rode that stage today with her bag full of murder money."

A dinner bell clanged inside and Ike Billings's boots hit the porch floor with an energetic plump. "It's about time!" he said. "Soon as I eat you can tell me more about it, young fella."

He got to his feet and headed gustily for the dining room.

CHAPTER XXII

It would take the man an hour to eat and Verne was in no temper to dally for even ten minutes. He crossed the street to Emery's saloon and questioned the bartender. "Belle Plover just drove a rig up the Pioneerville trail. Got any idea where she'd be going?"

"I got *two* ideas," the man said. Verne's guess was that as a competitor of Belle's he'd have no inclination to cover up for her. "Number one," the man said, "she maybe went after a load of moonshine. Number two, she's maybe deliverin' red-eye to some mine up in the woods. A lot of her trade comes that way."

"Did you see her leave?"

"Yep. At the livery barn she switched from the stage to a buggy, then stopped a few minutes at her saloon. She was in there only long enough to change her clothes. Then she came out and drove up the Pioneerville road."

"What about the suitcase she came in on the stage with? Did she take it into her saloon and leave it there?"

"She went into the saloon empty-handed," the man remembered, "and came out the same way."

To Verne it meant that her stagecoach baggage, transferred to the buggy at the livery barn, must have remained in the buggy when the woman drove off into the woods. "I understand she owns an abandoned mine called the Flying Dutchman."

"Could be," the bartender said. "Busted down mines are a dime a dozen around here. I got two or three no-good titles myself."

"Is the Flying Dutchman in the direction of Pioneerville?"

"Come to think of it, it is."

"Could I find my way there in the dark?"

"You could, but I wouldn't try it. If someone's makin' moonshine at that old mine shaft and hears you ridin' up in the dark, he might take you for a revenuer and start blastin' with buckshot. If I was you I'd wait till mornin', then take Sheriff Ike along."

"I'd hate to disturb his breakfast," Verne said. "How can I find that mine in the dark?"

"You take the Pioneerville trail toward Grimes Creek. It runs west past Boot Hill. You can't miss it because ore wagons have made deep ruts. About two mile past Boot Hill you come to a boarded-up roadhouse with a sluice flume by it. A run of fast water comes in from the north and it makes enough noise to guide you day or night. There's a dim wagon trail up that run that ain't been used for years. Only a mile of it till you come to the Flyin' Dutchman shafthouse. Been nothin' there but spiders and pack rats since the mine shut down. But if Belle Plover *did* drive out there you'll likely see a lamplight in the shack. Or maybe you'll meet her as she comes back."

Verne went out and hurried to the livery barn. "Saddle my roan," he directed.

In ten more minutes he was riding westerly up a wagon road which led to the mining settlements of Pioneersville, Centerville and Placerville. He'd been told that most of the county's gold production came from those three settlements, although in ever-lessening quantities.

Twilight faded and stars were out by the time Verne rode past Boot Hill. Rows of weedy mounds each with a weathered headboard were fenced on his right. Beyond, a forest of tall conifers swallowed the trail. They made a walled lane only wide enough for the wagon ruts which wound steeply upgrade.

"It's fishy, Blue," Verne muttered as he jogged on.

For Belle's buggy ride tonight didn't fit either of the reasons ascribed to it. She'd be tired and hungry after a day in the jolting stagecoach. To drive off into the woods without eating supper would need a more urgent reason than either of those mentioned. If she'd brought a large amount of money with her on the stage she might plan to bury it at the Flying Dutchman, or she could be taking it to someone—someone she could trust.

The woman had two outlaw brothers, Gabe and Gil. Gabe had been run out of Idaho long ago.

Gil was a fugitive from a recent Montana killing. Was Gil using Belle's mine shack for a hideout? To Verne the idea seemed much more plausible than that she'd rushed off to deliver or collect liquor.

About two miles past Boot Hill he saw the hulk of a boarded-up building loom by the road. Near it a sluice flume slanted from high ground toward the trail and here was a splash of fast water. A post had a sign tacked to it and to read it Verne struck a match. *GRIMES CREEK, 4 MILES.* An arrow pointed northwest.

A dim trail left the ore road and turned off up the running water. Verne dismounted and struck another match. Bending low he was able to make out fresh hoof marks and the tracks of buggy tires. They went up the creeklet. There were no return tracks. It convinced him that Belle Plover had driven to the Flying Dutchman and was still there.

Only a mile, according to the saloonman. Verne decided to walk it, leading the roan. That way he'd make less noise and could better see the trail.

It led him up an easy grade and followed close to the creeklet. The creek sound helped guide him. A mile would take twenty minutes and in any one of those minutes he might meet Belle coming back. Verne's saddle scabbard had a carbine but he left it there, choosing to depend on his holster gun. Darkness would mean close quarters if it came to a gunfight with Gil or Gabe, or with Belle herself. He had no doubt but that the woman was armed and could be as deadly, on a dark trail, as any gunman.

The twenty minutes seemed endless. The fir trees made tall, slim spires with down-slanting branches, shutting out starlight. Gravel, and sometimes a pine cone, crunched under Verne's feet. But the sounds were covered by the noise of fast water.

Rounding a curve of the path he saw lamplight. It came from a window and made a square of yellow against the blackness ahead. "Here's where I leave you, Blue." Verne tied the roan to a sapling and moved on alone, drawing the forty-five from its holster.

The lampglow was nearer than he'd thought. Suddenly it was close in front of him and the shapes of a cabin, a shafthouse and a winch were there too. A buggy was in front of the cabin, its one horse standing cock-kneed in the traces. "Whoa boy!" Verne whispered warily.

A whinny could give him away.

He got under the window and raised his eyes to the sill. She was there all right. The woman he'd never seen before but whose voice he'd heard in room 200. A woman of middle age with tawny hair and bags under her eyes. The room had a cot, and a packing box and a table with an oil lamp on it. A small man, shabby and shaggy, sat on the cot with a cigaret hanging from his lip and a gun holstered at his hip. Belle Plover sat on the packing box with a cup of beer by her. Half the window pane had been smashed out by hailstones and her words came plainly to Verne.

"Soon as I can sell the saloon, Gil, I'll meet you in El Paso."

"I'll be there," the man promised, "and we'll hit for Mexico City."

"We'd better go separate ways," Belle planned. "I'll go by way of Kelton and you by way of Winnemucca."

"You sure you ain't bein' watched?"

"Not me." Belle sipped her beer. "They don't even suspect Canby." She laughed harshly. "You should have seen him when he coughed up the money. Looked like he'd just had all his teeth pulled. Begged me to let him keep half of it and I told him to go to hell."

Gil Henry spat out his cigaret, grinning. "Must've scared the guts outa him."

"I had him where the hair was short, Gil, what with wedding bells less than a week away. 'You'll get it all back and more too,' I told him, 'when you marry that widow.'" The woman's eyes shifted to the door at the rear. "When are you goin' to do it, Gil?"

"Soon as you're gone. I can drop him down the shaft."

"Not this one," Belle cautioned. "I happen to own it. Better take him to the old McGuffey claim. It's a deeper shaft and only a mile up the hill."

The blunt callousness of it sickened Verne. He kicked the door open and walked in on them with his gun level. "There's been a change of plans," he announced. "You're not going anywhere except to jail. Hold it, Gil! Don't try anything."

Gil was on his feet with his hand on the grip of his gun. Panic froze Belle's flabby face as she sat rigidly on the packing box. The only sound was a click as Verne thumbed back the hammer of his forty-five.

The oil lamp was only a foot or so to Belle's right. Suddenly her hand slapped at it, toppling it with a crash of glass to the floor. As the room went dark she screamed: "Get him, Gil!"

Gil fired and Verne fired, both in jet darkness. A second shriek from Belle echoed the shots, like the scream of a leaping panther as she threw herself at Verne Hallam. In the dark he felt her fingers clawing at his face and her weight dragging him down.

No sound came from Gil Henry except a thump as he hit the floor. Verne's aim, which had been level and exact before the crash of the lamp, had given him an advantage over the blind draw and snap shot in the dark by Gil. Only the woman clawed at Verne now and with a desperate wrench he managed to free himself from her. As she came screaming at him again he swung the gun barrel at her twice, in the darkness missing the first swing.

His second caught her skull and he heard her fall.

When he'd struck a match and relighted the lamp they were both on the floor, the man dead and the woman in a wild hysteria of panic and hate. "Shut up," Verne said.

He crossed to an inner door and jerked it open. Beyond it, on a pile of burlap rags, lay the prisoner bound hand and foot. "Come, Mr. Lindsay," Verne Hallam said to him. "I'm taking you home to your wife."

CHAPTER XXIII

Two sealed reports were on the stage for Boise City when it left at seven in the morning. With them went a Wells Fargo package containing ten thousand dollars. Verne himself didn't go. "I'll take Lindsay down tomorrow," he told Sheriff Ike Billings. "We'll need all day to talk him into going at all."

"Afraid his wife won't want him back, huh?" Billings suggested. "Him duckin' out on her for ten years and now showin' up lookin' like a peeled onion. We'll let the barber work on him and see if we can slick him up a little."

One of the reports which went south on the stage was signed by Verne Hallam. It was a precise account of his encounter with Gil Henry and Belle Plover, and was addressed to Sheriff Oldham. A postscript said:

Please notify Nan Stanley at the Overland Hotel and ask her to notify Mrs. Lindsay.

The other report was from sheriff to sheriff:

Oldham,
Sheriff, Ada County:
Meet me at the county line at noon tomorrow, July 7. Will deliver to you

258

there one prisoner, Belle Henry Plover, charged with complicity in the kidnapping of Marcus Lindsay and of collecting ten thousand dollars cash as payment therefor. Said cash, found in her possession and believed to be part of the Bonanza loot, goes to you with this report. Recommend that you arrest Wade Canby, charging him with grand theft and the murder of Ross Jackson. Body of Gil Henry is being held here. Hallam and Lindsay will go down tomorrow by private conveyance.

Billings,
Sheriff, Idaho City.

All day July sixth, while a barber labored over Marcus Lindsay and Verne Hallam coaxed and cajoled to overcome the man's shyness, Sheriff Billings held court on the hotel porch. With his boots propped on the rail, a sandwich in one hand and a schooner of beer in the other, over and over he told the story of Marcus Lindsay, back from the dead after ten years, to a growing crowd of the curious from up and down More's and Grimes Creeks. Not often did a sensation like this one break in Idaho City. "Ain't been nothin' like it," he told them, "since they lynched the bogus dust passers at Wahoe Ferry."

"It'll stand Boise City on its ears, Ike, when they get that report of yours."

"Time was," Billings remembered, "when I could have sent it by wire."

Those were the days of Indian raids and big gold shipments when a telegraph line had been maintained between the two county seats. Now it was no longer necessary to call troops from Boise to put down Indian troubles, and bullion shipments were few and moderate. When a storm last winter had wrecked the wire line no-one had bothered to repair it.

"But they'll get my report by sundown," Billings said. "Looks like Oldham'll have a full house, time he pens up Canby and the Plover woman along with all them Massacre Canyon killers and Lew Rogan. I took over Lew's constable job here when he got fired, remember?"

Only twice that day did Ike Billings take his feet off the rail. Once at noon when the dinner bell rang and again when it rang for supper.

Ike Billings was brisk enough when at sunrise the next morning he drove a buckboard south out of town. Belle Plover, sullen and silent and handcuffed, sat on the seat by him. Behind them came a second rig bearing Verne Hallam and Marcus Lindsay. Two saddle horses were tied to the endgate as Verne whipped to a trot, keeping pace with the rig ahead.

"We oughta make the halfway house by eleven o'clock," Billings called back, "and the county line by noon."

They left the high open basin and wheeled into More's Creek Canyon. With each passing mile Marcus Lindsay looked more and more like he wanted to jump out and disappear into the fir forest which hemmed them on either side. "I've got no business bustin' in on her like this!"

"Buck up," Verne said. "You're a husband and a father, and it's time to go home."

"Not me," Lindsay fretted. "I'm not fit for a woman to look at. I should've stayed dead."

"Suppose you had!" Verne Hallam argued. "Suppose you hadn't left Utah. What would happen? A wedding would happen. Lois would be getting married to a sneak killer! That's what you're saving her from and by this time she knows it. Leaving everything else aside she's bound to be plenty grateful. Except for you she'd be in about the worst mess a woman can get in— hitching herself to a crook."

"It's no worse than being hitched to a scarecrow."

"It's a million times worse," Verne retorted.

The riffles of More's Creek murmured gently by the trail and presently they crossed a plank bridge. "What made you know who I am?" Lindsay wondered.

"Two burros named Tom and Jerry. Same name

you gave the Stanley mules." Verne told him about the Fourth of July parade in which Lois and the boy had driven the burro cart. "They do it every year. And next year you'll be in it yourself, proud as Punch. You've been missin' a lot, fella."

"I hear she's rich. What would she want with an old scarred-up tramp like me?"

"Yeh, she's rich," Verne agreed. "She got that way by trading your Squaw Creek claim for another one at Rocky Bar that happened to pay off big. So you started it all yourself." He looked critically at the man beside him. "That country barber did a pretty good job on you yesterday. Helps a lot, trimming your beard like that."

On the long drive from Kelton the man calling himself John Gresham had worn a bushy beard to cover as much as possible of his scarred face. But yesterday's barber had been smart enough to know that a neatly-trimmed beard and a short-cropped mustache would cover just as much flesh and be much more flattering. Under the brim of a new Stetson purchased yesterday only the lower half of his forehead and the upper half of his face was exposed. It was his wife's first sight of him that Lindsay most dreaded. By keeping his hat on he hoped to lessen the shock a little.

"What counts is a man's eyes," Verne argued. "And yours are as good as anybody's."

"I thought I'd lost them," the man said. "I mean right after the blast I thought I'd be blind. It was a big reason for not coming back. When I got to seeing good I figured it was too late."

"It's never too late to do the right thing."

Sheriff Billings was getting too far ahead and Verne used the whip to catch up. A northbound wagon met and passed them, its driver gaping at the hand-cuffed woman. "Ain't that Belle Plover?" he asked as he came opposite Verne.

Verne nodded and drove on. They came presently to Halfway House where the daily stages nooned and changed horses. From here it was only about an hour to the Ada County line. "I'll be back by one o'clock, Jethro," Ike Billings shouted to the stationmaster. "Have a mess of lamb chops ready for me, and some scrambled eggs and hot sourdough if you've got any."

Jethro waved jovially. "And a pitcher of beer, Ike. See you in two hours."

The two rigs rolled on, crossing the creek twice more. Then Billings turned his head to shout back, "County line's right around the next bend, boys."

It was a wide place in the canyon at the mouth of a gulch. As Verne trotted his team around the bend he saw two rigs waiting there. One was an open buckboard and the other was a two-horse top buggy. Deputy Ben Alanson stood by the buckboard. A woman and a small boy were getting out of the buggy.

A subdued excitement possessed the woman.

The boy wore knee pants and a butterfly bow tie. He had a scrubbed and starched look like a boy on his way to Sunday School.

Verne heard Lindsay catch his breath. With an involuntary reflex the mans arm went up in front of his face, as though dodging a blow. "It's Lois!" he whispered.

"Wait here, Mark," the woman said to the boy. She walked slowly toward Hallam's rig, stopping when she was halfway there to stare at the bearded man wearing the Stetson hat with the brim tipped forward. From her expression Verne could see that she wasn't at all sure that what they'd told her was true.

For half a minute no word was spoken. Then Verne nudged Lindsay with an elbow. "Go to her. Don't let her stand there alone."

With Billings and Alanson and Hallam and Belle Plover and the nine-year-old boy looking on, Marcus Lindsay got out of the rig and moved forward. He walked with his head erect, his shoulders square, his eyes level as they met his wife's. Three steps from her he stopped. A sudden strange courage made him take off the hat he'd meant for a shield, exposing the blackened skin of his hairless scalp and showing him at his worst.

Lois Lindsay kept staring at him, and in a moment doubt as to whether he was her husband became a certainty that he wasn't. "You're a complete stranger," she decided with conviction.

"I reckon I am, Lois," the man answered humbly.

His voice made all the difference. That and the straightforward blueness of his eyes made her gasp breathlessly. "Say that again, please."

He said it again, and more. "I didn't know about the boy. Not till two months ago at Salt Lake. Then I came for a look at him. And at you. But I didn't figure for you to see me. I meant to be long gone by now."

His voice and his simple sincerity reversed a certainty and she knew he was Marcus Lindsay. The instant she was sure a change in her confused Verne. Whatever it was, she covered it with a forced formality. Verne saw her turn and beckon to the boy. When he came to stand by her she said: "This is your father, Mark. Mark, this is your son."

The man put the hat back on his head. "Hello, Mark."

"I am very glad to know you, sir," the boy said.

The man and the woman still stood three paces apart, equally restrained. There was no embrace, no tears, only what seemed to be a formal acceptance of fact. And all at once Verne Hallam knew why. The embarrassment wasn't all Lindsay's. In the first few minutes of shock the woman's could hardly be less than the man's. She'd buried him. In three more days she would have married his would-be murderer. Lindsay's sense of guilt and apology was for his truancy of ten years. Whatever matching sense of guilt ruled Lois Lindsay she covered it by saying to the boy: "Would you like to ride with Mr. Hallam, Mark?"

Verne being Mark's cowboy hero, an affirmative needed no coaxing. Lois took him by the hand and led him to the forewheel of Verne's rig. When he'd scrambled up to the seat his mother walked around to the driver's side. "Lean over, Verne," she said.

When Verne did, she kissed him on the cheek. "Thank you for bringing back my husband."

Then she went to the man she hadn't seen for ten years and took his arm. "Will you drive me home, Marcus?"

The two walked silently to the buggy and Marcus Lindsay helped her into it. He got in himself, took the reins, pulled the team through a half circle and the rig rolled briskly toward Boise City.

The pair of sheriffs, the cowboy and the prisoner gazed after them. In a moment Belle Plover looked at Verne Hallam with a brazen smirk. "You're the only one that got kissed, cowboy. Can't say's I blame her, with that face of his."

"We got to give her time to get used to it," Alanson said. "Right now it's time for you to change rigs, Belle."

When the hand-cuffed woman had been shifted to the Ada County vehicle, Ike Billings turned his buckboard around. "They're waitin' dinner for me up the road. Giddap." He drove smartly up More's Creek in the direction from which he'd come.

Ben Alanson delayed starting and twisted a cigaret. "Let's not try to catch up with 'em, Verne. Leave 'em lead the parade into town. The guy hired out at Kelton to drive a rig into Boise City. He's a little late, and it's not the same rig, but it looks like he'll get there just the same."

"Have they nabbed Lew Rogan?" Verne asked.

"Yep. Caught him hiding in a loft near Middleton."

"What about Canby?"

"No luck with Canby. The Idaho City news leaked out before we could pick him up, and he vamoosed. We looked in his room, his office, in every bar, hotel and rooming house in town. Searched every stagecoach, freight outfit and immigrant wagon leaving on all roads and he just ain't anywhere. Looks like he's clean gone." Alanson took the seat beside his prisoner and cracked his whip. "I'll take the lead, Hallam. You follow me into town."

CHAPTER XXIV

They didn't catch sight of the buggy for an hour. Then Verne got a glimpse of it crawling up the Robie Creek grade where all horses had to be held to a walk. The buggy's top being up, the two in it couldn't be seen from the rear.

"Wonder what they're sayin' to each other," Alanson called back to Verne.

Verne, only a length behind, heard a cynical laugh from Belle Plover. "I bet she wishes to hell he'd stayed dead."

Neither Verne nor Alanson answered the woman. But the boy Mark did and his voice was shrilly indignant. "No such thing. She wants him back just like I do."

"Sure she does," Verne said.

"If you open your dirty mouth again," Alanson said to Belle, "I'll stuff a rag in it."

The buggy disappeared over Shaw's Mountain Gap and soon the others were following it down the barren twists of Cottonwood Gulch.

"Will they hang Mr. Canby?" the boy asked abruptly.

"That's not for us to say," Verne answered gravely. "Who told you about it, Mark?"

"No-one. But I heard the milkman tell Helga."

Helga, Verne remembered, was the Swedish

servant. "You mean when he delivered milk this morning you heard him talk to Helga in the kitchen?"

The boy nodded. "They didn't see me come in. He told Helga that Mr. Canby killed Mr. Jackson to get the money to pay Gil Henry to kill my father."

It would have been told to Lois Lindsay, perhaps by Nan or Warren Stanley, perhaps by some old friend like John Hailey, in terms less brutal than that. But the sense of it would have been much the same.

What a shattering shock must have hit the woman late yesterday! A revelation so hard to believe that today she'd driven to the county line with Alanson to verify with her own eyes and ears the identity of a man who'd called himself John Gresham. And once she knew for sure he was Marcus Lindsay there'd come a stab of remorse for the hideous mistake she'd made ten years ago, and with it the scourge of shame for planning to marry Wade Canby.

All of that, Verne thought, must have preyed on the woman's sensibilities as she'd stood face to face with Marcus Lindsay. It would build inside of her a humility no less than his own.

But now they'd ridden thirteen miles together, down a piney canyon, up and over a mountain, on toward Boise City, where they'd parted ten years ago. What, Verne wondered, were they saying to each other behind the screen of the buggy top?

As the sun dipped lower the roofs of the capital came in sight and presently, at its northeastern outskirts, the buggy stopped and waited. It was at a fork of streets near the mouth of Cottonwood Gulch. The street ahead would take them to the business district; by turning to the left they could strike the residential section on Warm Springs Avenue.

Verne drew up beside the buggy. The man and woman in it seemed relaxed, now. Neither seemed self-conscious or afraid of the other. Thirteen miles had worked some magic of healing and the lilt of it was in Lois's voice as she called to her boy. "Come, Mark. Here's where we Lindsays turn off."

The boy jumped out of Verne's rig and got into the buggy. Lois Lindsay, sitting between her husband and her son, waved a goodbye. "You and Nan come to see us some time, Verne Hallam."

Then they were gone down an elm-shaded lane which would take them quickly home.

With two saddle horses tied to his endgate, Verne drove on and at Eighth and Bannack turned in at Agnew's stable. "It's an Idaho City rig," he said. "Send it back the first chance you get."

By the time he'd walked a block to the jail Belle Plover had been lodged behind bars. A crowd was clamoring for details but Verne managed to avoid everyone except Sheriff Oldham, Orlando Robbins and a *Statesman* reporter. To these he filled in the gaps in the report sent down by Ike Billings.

Oldham clapped him on the back. "You've got three thousand dollars coming to you, boy. And you sure earned it."

Verne stared. "Three thousand dollars?"

"No less. A two thousand dollar reward posted by Montana for Gil Henry, dead or alive. On top of that, the Bonanza here offered ten per cent for the return of all or any part of the fourteen thousand Canby stuck 'em up for. You recovered ten thousand of it."

"You haven't picked up Canby yet?"

"Nope. He faded into thin air. How he got outa town nobody knows. His horse is still in the stable and there's no record that he bought or rented or stole another one. Wherever he is, he's still got four thousand of that Bonanza money."

Verne finally got away and made for the Overland Hotel. It was twilight, with the sidewalks full. Many persons tried to waylay Verne and buy him a drink. The story of Lindsay's rescue was on every tongue in town. Verne brushed them aside and hurried on, fairly sure that Nan would be at the Overland with one or both of her brothers.

In the lobby he found Paul Stanley. "Where's that wagon driver of ours?" Paul demanded buoyantly. "Between the two of you, you've made the Stanley outfit famous."

"Lindsay's doing all right. Where's Nan?"

"Up in her room," Paul confided, "making herself pretty for you. You can tell us all about it at supper."

"Us?"

"Nan and Warren and Florence and me."

"Who's Florence?"

"An army girl Warren met at the Fourth of July parade. He's got a supper date with her and they're up in the parlor right now. Nan'll join us there."

Verne went first to his own room, where he shaved and changed his shirt. He brushed his wavy russet hair and shined his boots, then hurried down the hall to the small upstairs parlor. The Stanley brothers were there with a slender brunette from Fort Boise and it was at once clear to Verne that Warren's interest in her was more than casual. "We're going to show Florence the ranch tomorrow," Warren said jubilantly.

"I believe I met you at the post dance, Mr. Hallam," the army girl remembered. "You told me you were on your way to Oregon."

"I must've been crazy," Verne said. "What's wrong with Idaho?"

Nan came into the parlor and he immediately forgot the rest of them. She had on the full-skirted dance frock of pale yellow she'd worn at the Fort Boise ball. Her cheeks had roses and her eyes had stars as Verne took both of her hands. "Gosh, Nan!"

He was trying to find the right words to tell Nan how beautiful she was when the army girl broke in smoothly: "We'll wait for you downstairs." She tucked one hand under Warren's arm and another under Paul's, leading them out of the parlor. Verne heard them going down to the lobby.

"You *did* say you were going to Oregon," Nan reminded him.

"I did? But Idaho'd suit me right good, if . . ."

"If what?"

"If I could get that relinquishment," Verne said.

"What's a relinquishment?"

"It's a release on a partly proved-up home-stead," he explained. "Say a man files on land and starts to improve it. But before the three years are up he decides he doesn't want to go on with it. The law allows him to relinquish his rights for whatever he can get—which generally is about what the improvements cost him. The relinquishment buyer can then re-file the tract under his own name and prove up."

"So?" Nan prompted. He hadn't let go of her hands yet.

"So Jim Agnew was telling me about a relinquishment for sale right across the Boise River from Middleton. A fenced quarter with a three-room cabin on it. It's only a few miles below your place, Nan. Thought I'd go down there tomorrow for a look."

"I hope you like it," Nan murmured.

"I hope *you* like it too. Will you go there with me tomorrow?"

"Yes."

"And right now will you let me kiss you?"

"Yes."

Verne kissed her. "That's only a start. Soon as I collect a couple of rewards, will you marry me?"

"Only on one condition."

"Name it."

"That you make a relinquishment yourself. Your deputy job or any job that makes you wear a gun. I don't want a husband who's always getting shot at. Promise me that after today you'll never again wear a gun."

"I promise." Verne kissed her again. "Never again after today."

Hand in hand they went down to join the others.

CHAPTER XXV

The lobby clock said eleven when the party broke up. Verne went to his room walking on air. At supper they'd said nothing to the others about an engagement—only that they were going down river tomorrow to look at a relinquishment.

Their very act of looking at a relinquishment made them landseekers, and homeseekers. The army girl's single syllable "Oh!" expressed that subtle perception—as did a narrowing of Warren's eyes and a broad smile from Paul. There was an exchange of quips, light on the surface but full of meaning: Paul's, "First thing you know we'll be needing a new housekeeper, Warren"; and Warren's, "I've already got one in mind, Paul."

Then Nan's fast shift to another subject. "Speaking of relinquishments, there'll never be a match for the one Marcus Lindsay made ten years ago. But now he's getting it back again. Tell us what they said to each other, Verne."

To Verne it made no great difference whether the down river relinquishment looked good or bad. What counted was that Nan was going with him to look at it. It meant that she'd already become the partner of his life.

He was taking off his boots when someone

knocked at the door of his room. It might be Warren or Paul, or maybe it was some new word from Oldham at the jail.

With one boot on and one off Verne went to the door and opened it. Doctor Eph Smith stood there, satchel in hand. He came in and Verne closed the door. "Had to make a call down the hall, so I thought I'd pop in a minute for a look at that lump on your head."

"It's ancient history," Verne grinned. He sat on the bed while Eph Smith gave a look. Only three nights had passed since he'd put this patient to sleep with a double sedative.

"You've been lucky," the doctor said. "But it can't keep up forever. I speak from long observation, boy. Gun-wearers and sheriffs die young."

"That's what my girl says," Verne admitted. "She made me promise to hang up my gun for keeps after today."

"Shows she's got sense. This territory's full of young widows who made the mistake of letting their husbands run around with posses and trading bullets with outlaws like Plover and Gil Henry. Most of them end up like young Bud Akins and Chuck Prather, six feet under before they're twenty-three years old. Well, goodnight, boy. You know where my office is, if you ever get a bellyache, or anything." He breezed out of the room.

Verne sat down and took off the other boot. He was about to drop it when an echo of Eph Smith's last words hung provocatively in his mind. *"You know where my office is."*

Yes, I know now, Verne remembered; *but there was a time when I didn't!*

A decoy calling himself Baker had lured him to an empty house on Grove Street, after putting Eph Smith's shingle on the gate.

Was that house still empty? Had Oldham's crew searched it for Wade Canby?

They'd looked in saloons and rooming houses, barn lofts and outbound stagecoaches, but had they thought to search the empty house?

It would make a perfect hiding place for Canby. It was an hour before midnight on the seventh of July. Billings's report on Canby's guilt had reached here about sundown on the sixth, some thirty hours ago. The Grove Street house was only two blocks from Canby's office in the Stone Jug. Where quicker could he disappear to?

By hiding there for a night or two till the hue and cry subsided a little, he might hope to slip away under cover of darkness, and escape for good. He could be there at this very moment— and be gone before morning!

A nagging urge to find out kept Verne from dropping his second boot. Instead, he put it back on and the other boot too. He slipped on his jacket, then reached for a gunbelt. The jacket was the one he'd worn at Idaho City and still had a deputy's badge pinned on it.

The badge and the gunbelt made him remember his promise. He'd promised Nan he'd leave manhunting to others. If he went to the Grove Street house looking for Canby he'd be breaking that promise.

Or would he? It wasn't midnight yet. *After today,* he'd told Nan. And today would last another fifty minutes.

In any case there was no harm in finding out if the house was still empty. Maybe honest tenants had moved in by now. In a very few minutes he could relieve his mind about the matter.

Verne buckled on the gunbelt and tied the holster cord to his right thigh. Then he turned the lamp low and hurried down to the street. Two blocks east along Main took him to the Stone Jug at Sixth. Jauman's bar on the ground floor was lighted but otherwise the building was dark. Verne paused for a moment in front of steps leading to the upper offices. Canby's office was at the head of those stairs. But the man wouldn't dare hide there. It was the first place a sheriff would look.

Grove was the next street south of Main and the empty house was only half a block to the left on it. Verne hurried there, and one look convinced him that the house still had no tenant. It loomed dark and shuttered beyond its front yard pickets.

A narrow, gabled house two stories high, it appeared quite as it had on Verne's first nightly visit except that now Eph Smith's shingle was gone.

Was Wade Canby skulking back of those shutters?

There was only one way to find out. Verne advanced to the front door, tried it and found it locked. So was a porch window whose dusty shutters clearly hadn't been disturbed.

Verne Hallam circled the house, looking at all the downstairs windows. A door at the back was locked, but a window by it wasn't. This window, giving on a covered porch, had no shutters. The glass pane had been partially knocked out and the catch beyond it wasn't latched.

Someone, maybe a tramp seeking shelter, maybe a fugitive like Canby, could have smashed the glass, then reached through to release the catch.

Verne raised the sash and climbed in. After striking a match he saw that he was in a stoveless kitchen with an iron hand pump on its sink. A wetness under the pump's spout meant that it had been used recently—probably to draw water from the cistern. Many Idaho houses had kitchen pumps. Verne saw two apple cores on the sink and remembered seeing an apple tree in the back yard.

He'd used several matches before he found a

pair of candles in the kitchen cabinet. He lighted both, standing each in a saucer. He left one of them burning on the sink and, using the other for a torch, he began exploring the house.

His left hand held the candle and his right the forty-five gun as he moved forward up the hallway. There were no carpets, no furniture, only dusty pine floors. A warped floor board creaked under Verne's weight. He moved stealthily on to the front, where the two outlaws had gun-whipped him on his first visit here. Those gun-whippers along with Frank Hugo had rescued Schulte and Joad from a stagecoach in Massacre Canyon. All five were now in jail but it wouldn't bring back to life two boyish deputies named Akins and Prather. Deputies die young, said Eph Smith.

The candlelight showed no-one in the parlor nor in any other of the ground floor rooms.

If the prowler who'd broken a window was still here he was upstairs. Verne began moving up those stairs, candle in one hand and gun in the other. Halfway up, again a board creaked under his weight.

From above came a sound which seemed to be a faint scampering at the end of the upper hallway—possibly a mouse. After a minute of silence Verne went up, step by step. At the top his candlelight showed him four doors, three closed and one open.

He moved first to the open doorway and looked in. It was a square, high-ceilinged room, entirely bare. The dust on the floor showed no footprints. There was a closet, but in it Verne found only a moth-eaten, castaway coat.

Returning to the hallway he moved from door to door of the other three bedrooms. None of the doors was locked. None of the rooms was occupied. But in the last of the three he found an apple core. Whoever had intruded into this house seemed to have fed himself on apples.

But this was only the seventh of July, too early for Idaho apples to be ripe. This core was not only ripe, but over-ripe, in fact almost spoiled.

So it was an apple from last fall's crop. It gave Verne an idea and he returned to the lower hallway, groping along it for a basement door. Often a house had a basement bin used to store fruit over winter. Apples and potatoes were sometimes kept that way until a new season's crop could be harvested. Was there an apple bin under this house?

Hallway doors gave only onto closets, but in the kitchen Verne found one which opened to steep descending steps. He opened it a bit wider and held his torch through it, looking down on a cement floor at the bottom. What he saw made him draw quickly back into the kitchen.

Someone was down there. In his momentary survey of the basement Verne had glimpsed a cracker box with the stub of a candle set upright on it. The candle wasn't lighted but the fact that it was there suggested a hideaway. Verne had also noted an open bin hanging by wires from rafters and partly full of last year's apples. A man skulking down there, hearing Verne moving around above, would blow out his candle.

Who could it be but Wade Canby? Verne weighed the idea of going out to look for Constable Paxton. Or he could run to the sheriff's office five blocks away and report a prowler here.

But while I'm gone he'd slip away!

It was a chance Verne couldn't take. He blew out his candle and took off his boots. When the candle was cool he dropped it into his coat pocket. It left the kitchen dark—as dark as the cellar itself.

Verne groped through the basement doorway and felt with his bootless foot for the next step down. When he bore his weight on it, it didn't creak. Again he groped for a lower step. Tread by tread he went down, gun in hand and holding his breath. When he was nearly at the bottom his forehead bumped a ceiling rafter. Dust sprayed him and the shock of it made him take the last step too fast.

It put him off balance and he stumbled over the cracker box, falling across it just as a roar and a flash of gunfire came from beyond the apple bin. He managed to keep the grip on his gun as he rolled over twice, coming to a stop against a masonry foundation wall. Wade Canby was down there with him! Canby cornered and desperate to shoot his way out. The man wasn't a practiced gunman like Plover or Hugo or Gil Henry. But here the blackness made all men equal.

Verne got quietly to his feet and made ready to shoot at any flash or sound. Minutes slipped by and none came. What would Canby do in a trap like this?

He'll try to feel his way to the steps and get out. Verne aimed his gun toward where he thought the steps were. He remembered Gil and Belle in the mine cabin, two nights ago. *Why must I always fight them in the dark?*

A thud came from the steps, halfway up, then the sounds of something bouncing back down to the basement floor. The man had thrown an apple to draw Verne's fire. The gun-flash would expose Verne's position. Not long ago Verne had tried the same trick himself in his own darkened room at the Overland.

It proved that the man was within easy reach of the apple bin. Verne stood silently in his stocking feet with his back to the masonry wall. He groped to his left and found no obstacle within arm's reach in that direction. Then he leveled his gun and fired approximately toward the bin, guided only by his memory. With the shot he stepped quickly a full pace to his left.

Another roar and flash answered his shot, chipping stone from the wall where he'd stood and stenching the cellar with smoke. Marking the flash, Verne fired twice at it and a cry from the dark meant a hit. The man didn't shoot back.

The next sound was a moan of pain at the floor level, beyond the fruit bin. With his gun still level Verne took a chance and lighted a match.

When it didn't draw fire he knew that the man was down and helpless. He dropped the nearly spent match and lighted another, moving warily forward. At the base of the bin he found Wade Canby on hands and knees, groping for the gun which had slid away from him. "You won't need it," Verne said.

He took the candle from his pocket and lighted it. Blood at Canby's right ear meant that his legs were all right. "Get up and walk."

He prodded the man to his feet. There was no fight in Canby now. Bulges in his pockets made Verne suspect another gun. But when he searched the pockets he found only money—four packets of twenty-dollar bills, with fifty in each packet. In all four thousand dollars, the rest of the Bonanza take after paying off Belle Plover.

It was a long five blocks to the jail. Walking Canby there under the stares of saloon customers, who tumbled out at the fast-spreading story of the man's capture, took nearly half an hour. Many offered to help but Verne, remembering that men like these had made up a lynch crowd only three nights ago, brushed them aside.

Alone he marched Canby up Sixth to Idaho and west on Idaho to Eighth. There was no time to treat the bullet cut that had sheared off half of Canby's ear. Canby was in screaming torture when Verne pushed him into the jail office.

Ben Alanson and a night jailer were on duty. "Here's the rest of his take," Verne said. He dropped the four thousand dollars on Oldham's desk.

Alanson gaped at Canby, then at the money. "Where the devil did you find him?"

"In the dark—where he's lived most of his life," Verne said.

The jailer took over Canby and led him to a cell.

Alanson came out of his trance and cocked a calculating eye at the money. "Ten per cent'll give you another four hundred dollars, cowboy. What you gonna do with all that dough?"

"I figure to get married and start a ranch. Only I promised to get rid of these first." Verne took off his gunbelt and laid it, gun, holster and all, on the desk. Then he unpinned his deputy's badge and laid it beside the gun. "I'll make you a present of them, Ben."

Alanson stared blankly. "How you gonna run a ranch without a gun?"

"I've still got a rifle to keep house with. A married man has to make a few sacrifices, they say."

Verne Hallam left the jail and hurried to the Overland Hotel, entering there on the stroke of midnight. The long day was over now, and tomorrow would begin a new one with Nan.

Books are produced in the United States using U.S.-based materials

Books are printed using a revolutionary new process called THINKtech™ that lowers energy usage by 70% and increases overall quality

Books are durable and flexible because of smythe-sewing

Paper is sourced using environmentally responsible foresting methods and the paper is acid-free

Center Point Large Print
600 Brooks Road / PO Box 1
Thorndike, ME 04986-0001 USA

(207) 568-3717

US & Canada:
1 800 929-9108
www.centerpointlargeprint.com